Tales from the Silver State II

Tales from the Silver State II

Short Fiction from Nevada's Freshest Voices

Noëlle de Beaufort

T.C. Contin • Steve Fey

John Hill • Patricia Kranish

Trina Kurilla • M. McCutcheon

Marshall Prescott • Craig A. Ruark

Jeffrey Segal • Barbra Wolfe

Edited by Richard J. Warren

Muddy Pig Press • Las Vegas, Nevada

Tales from the Silver State

Photo Credit: © Can Stock Photo Inc. / IamCDN

ISBN-13: 978-0692354070

ISBN-10: 0692354077

Printed in the United States of America

www.muddypigpress.com

Muddy Pig Press • Las Vegas, Nevada

Dedicated to the Memory
of Jay MacLarty

Every moment is a golden one for him who has the vision to recognize it as such. - Henry Miller

Table of Contents

Editors Note

By Richard J. Warren

The first edition of Tales from the Silver State was released in early 2014. The collection was assembled as a way to honor the legacy of Jay MacLarty, a Simon & Shuster author and founder of the Las Vegas Writers Group. Jay envisioned the group as a place where writers could come together to learn from one another and support each other as they practiced their craft. Many writers have passed through this group on their way to finding success as authors. Several of them were invited to contribute to that inaugural volume as a way to pay tribute to Jay.

The success of that first edition made the decision to publish a sequel an easy one. This year the more than three hundred members of the LVWG were invited to submit tales for this edition of the anthology. The many submissions were read anonymously by a panel of readers and the best stories were chosen for publication. Those are the tales you will read here.

Assembling an anthology would not be possible without the help and support of others. Acknowledgement and thanks to the contributing authors: Noëlle de Beaufort, T.C. Contin, Steve Fey, John Hill, Patricia Kranish, Trina Kurilla, M. McCutcheon, Marshall Prescott, Craig A. Ruark, Jeffrey Segal and Barbra Wolfe.

Special thanks to the creative writing faculty and students at the University of Nevada Las Vegas for their assistance with this project. As always, thanks to the "piglets" on staff at the Muddy Pig Press for making this anthology possible.

426 Miles

By Trina Kurilla

Four hundred and twenty-six miles into the drive, the aching in Charlotte's right foot started to become more persistent, so she toggled the cruise control on for a few minutes. Stretching her foot out, fantasies of a future foot massage crept into her mind. It had been awhile since she'd done such a long drive without anyone to switch off with, but she was determined to get to Las Vegas before it was even close to getting dark.

Charlotte had gotten an extremely early start. She thought the clock had said some time after four in the morning when she left, but she hadn't paid too much attention. She hadn't been able to sleep that night, the melatonin never kicked in, and the extra Zzz tea had passed through her quicker than she drank it. At a certain point she gave in to the fact she was having a sleepless weekend. She couldn't stop thinking about that piece of paper. First it had been in her wallet; every time she went to pull money out she could see the edge of the paper stick out past the money. Even if only a sliver was visible, her eyes would catch it. Putting it in her desk drawer had been no better; it taunted her every time she reached in for a pen.

Three months ago, she was meeting Ava for lunch when her old friend handed her a small box.

"You're five months early for my birthday, but I accept your thoughtful intentions." Amused, she brought the little box up to her ear and shook it, "It's awfully light, Ava. Did you forget to put something in here?"

Ava rolled her eyes and snatched the box back, "Come on, I'm not that absentminded," she held it for a moment before setting it on the table and pushing it toward Charlotte, "Just open it."

It was a plain white jewelry box with a ribbon tied around it, giving nothing up for what could be inside. Ava hadn't gone on a trip, so no reason to have brought her back anything. She reached for the box as apprehension clung to her fingers. Ava waited impatiently as she opened it; Charlotte could see her friend restraining herself from yanking the box away to open it herself. Inside was a slip of paper with what looked like an out of state address. Bewildered, Charlotte looked to Ava for explanation.

"It's your birth mother's address."

Charlotte must have misheard her, "No, really. Ava, what is this?"

"I wouldn't joke with you about this. When we were growing up you talked about finding her all the time."

"I don't know if it was *all* the time…"

"I just did a little digging –"

"You're definitely good at that," Charlotte muttered.

"Look," Ava started, "I was just trying to do something nice. I'm sorry I looked it up…" disgruntled, she picked at her pasta.

Charlotte held the box in her hands, her food all but forgotten, "It's been so long since I've thought about her. I used to imagine her appearing outside in a car, telling me she was taking me away…that we'd be happy…driving off into the sunset. That usually happened when I was angry at my mom," a sad smile crossed her face and she glanced up at Ava to see she was listening, "but every kid does that. Did I ever tell you I dreamt about her?"

Ava shook her head.

"Well, at least I think it was her…my memory after waking up was never clear enough to describe in detail what I saw. As I got older the dreams didn't come as often, I had started looking forward to them, but the less I saw her the more I thought I was losing something…like I had done something bad to lose her in that way, too."

"Do you parents know about the dreams?" Ava asked tentatively.

"I told my mom about it once when I was really young. I think I was six, which led to this really big conversation about how some mommies will have babies for other mommies who can't have babies or sometimes mommies aren't ready for a baby, so they give the baby to parents that are."

"That's kind of heavy for a six year old."

"I didn't know it at the time, but that was their first attempt at being open about my adoption," she paused as the waiter came by to refill their water glasses, "I've been lucky, I know that. My parents have always been supportive, of course my mom and I fight, but who doesn't?"

"That's normal...for you two anyway. At least you're not like your aunt and cousin that used to fist fight each other."

"Used to? That hasn't stopped, it doesn't happen as often as when she was fifteen – but that's not my point. My life could be infinitely worse...but it's not," Charlotte said and put the lid back on the address, "As much as I wanted to know then..."

"You know, you wouldn't have to go alone, I would go with you. I did open this can of worms anyway." She said, stuffing her mouth with pasta.

Charlotte slid the box back over to Ava, "I don't know–"

"Keep it," she said, pushing it back, "We could make it a little vacation, discover your past, play some roulette, do some club hopping, drink to whether we regret coming, who knows..."

Charlotte's apprehension melted a little at Ava's attempt to break the tension, "Alright, I'll think about it," she said, accepting the box again.

Eventually, the slip of paper found its way out of the box and into places where Charlotte did her best not to acknowledge it. But seeing as it was currently tapped to the road atlas her parents had gifted her the previous Christmas, avoiding it hadn't worked. Her parents had persisted in showing her how to read maps growing up and nicknamed her Char the Navigator during their family trips. The habit stuck with her so well she was usually the one giving directions when she went places with friends. She'd tried using GPS before, but it wasn't nearly as fun using the map. It lay open on the passenger's seat; Charlotte had merged onto I-15 from I-70 awhile ago. She knew she'd be getting into St. George, Utah, in the next twenty minutes or so, it'd be good to try to get some food in her system.

The familiar sound of her cell phone interrupted her thoughts, and guilt moved to the front of her mind. Without looking, she knew it was probably Ava again. They were supposed to get manicures and pedicures today for a wedding they were going to be in the following Tuesday. But, over the course of twenty-four hours her apartment walls had started to close in on her and panic attacks had her sticking her face out of her windows; there just wasn't enough air. Staying put wasn't an option. She needed to find out once and for all. She scolded herself for her poor timing, but who plans to have a breakdown in an organized way? Reaching to tip over her phone in the cup holder, Ava's name was visible on the screen. Charlotte would call her back once she stopped driving.

After fueling up, Charlotte sat in a deserted parking lot, munching on sweet potato fries, and dialed Ava's number. She debated on her choice of fast food when a gurgle from her stomach told her where it stood on the matter.

Ava answered, "Hold on." The phone sounded far away as Charlotte heard Ava say she needed to step out for a minute to someone on her end, "Where the *hell* have you been? I go inside your apartment and you're nowhere to found, the car was gone from the garage, you don't answer your phone for hours, and Dustin has no clue where you are either. Your *own* man didn't even know you were gone. Kelly wouldn't get off my back until I made up some story that you were balls deep with a twenty-four flu bug."

"Well, you're not totally off base with the vomiting thing," she said as her stomach turned, planning an uprising.

"Charlotte." Her irritation clear.

Picking at one of her cuticles, "I just needed to leave, okay? I know you said you'd go with me, but after yesterday – I just realized I needed to go find her on my own."

"Well, damn..."

"Believe me, this is the last thing I expected to be doing today."

"I guess now's as good a time as any to do some soul searching, but seriously, you couldn't wait until after the free mani/pedi?"

"They're free?" Charlotte asked, surprised, "Since

when?"

"Since Kelly's stepdad's loaded."

"Sounds about right. Think they'll take pity on toilet-bound me and give me a belated free one?"

"Already taken care of," Ava responded.

A laugh found its way out of Charlotte's mouth, "You're something else."

"You're welcome. Wait a sec." Ava replied to muffled voices in the background, "Apparently my presence is being missed at *Ladies Tea Time*," Charlotte snickered at Ava's fake accent, "I get why you're doing this solo, but you're going to have to tell me later about why you fled like a thief in the night."

Charlotte didn't even know, "I should probably call Dustin anyway and let you get back to your finger sandwiches."

"Hey, they're actually good, I got to be one of the food testers remember? Anyway, go on, call your man...I think I freaked him out earlier."

"Oh really, couldn't tell," she said while cleaning the accumulated bugs off the car windows; remembering the series of deceptively calm texts from Dustin she had scrolled through earlier, "*What* did you say to him?"

"I can be a bit...*dramatic* sometimes..."

Charlotte cringed, but she was the one pulling the disappearing act, "I guess I deserve some backlash, I'll let you go."

"Be safe, alright?"

"What else would I be?" Charlotte could imagine Ava's stern expression, "I'll text you when I get to the hotel."

"That's what I like to hear," Ava said with enthusiasm.

Before Charlotte could retort, her friend hung up. Cursing at Ava under her breath, she plopped the phone back in the cup holder. Focusing on the drive, she tried to clear her mind. Ever since Ava had given her the address, she'd been isolating herself. Having abandoned getting answers to her questions long ago, things had resurfaced with the appearance of the address, to say the least it was overwhelming.

For the last few months she had stayed at Dustin's place less often, opting to read through her old journals, rediscovering her younger self. It had been strange to realize she hadn't changed as much as she thought. Growing up hadn't stripped away her insecurities, but a better appreciation for what she had emerged. What ifs about a different life with her birth mother faded because there was no changing what she had no control over, except now she did. Charlotte didn't want to know why she had been put up for adoption. More than anything she wanted to fill the hazy face from her dream with the original, to actually feel the warmth in her embrace, and see if the color in her first mother's eyes matched her own bright green, so different from her adopted parents' dull brown irises.

Dustin knew Charlotte was adopted, that she had struggled with her identity in her family even though they never acted as if she wasn't their biological child. What she had omitted from her concerned significant other was the location she was navigating to. The guilt for excluding him about Ava's detective work was reaching its peak.

No more avoiding the inevitable, her fingers found the quick-dial button for his number. The phone barely rang once before he answered it. After making sure there was no search party being drafted she assured him that she was just fine. Seeing highway patrol up ahead she put him on speakerphone, passing the cruiser without notice. His voice lost the panicked edge as they talked, but even so, she was glad he didn't know her parents numbers yet. Having them team up to find their lost, abducted, or otherwise maimed Charlotte was best avoided. While the anxiety in her own stomach eased as they talked, Charlotte knew she still owed Dustin an apology.

"I have to tell you something."

Charlotte sensed the shifting tension, even without being in the same room with him.

"Okay," his voice instantly apprehensive.

"I should have told you months ago, I just didn't know what to do, you know? Getting your birth mother's last known location dropped in your lap is not something I can just deal with easily...I didn't realize how much I still cared..."

Dustin was quiet and then he started to laugh, "Thank god, I thought you were going to break up with me. You've seemed so far away lately...I've been too afraid to ask you if

I've been doing something wrong."

"What?" Charlotte almost drifted into the next lane at the thought, "That is *so* far from what is going on. Jesus, I'm sorry, Dusty, I had no idea I was giving you that vibe. I've just been so freaked out about this. The only person that knew was Ava and that's because she's the one who found her, I couldn't tell my parents, and honestly...at first I wasn't sure I even wanted to know."

"I'm sorry you've felt so alone about this, but you know you don't have to deal with it alone, right? That's what I'm here for, have you thought about what you want to do? Do you want to go see her? If you want me to, I would go with you, I'm sure I can get time off at work."

"I know you would go with me and I'm so grateful for that," she smiled, "but this is something I need to do on my own...in fact, I'm doing it."

"We can talk about it when I get inside. I'm coming up the stairs right now."

"What do you mean?"

"I've got Jell-O, electrolytes, and Pepto Bismol for you in between sessions of you throwing-up and watching Patrick Swayze movies."

"Aww, you brought me Jell-O? How do you know Swayze is my go-to?"

"I'm here. Let me in."

"Dustin, I'm fifty-six miles away from Vegas right now; I'm going to meet my mom."

"Wait, aren't you sick or was that part of Ava's dramatic monologue?"

"Me being sick is the most truthful thing that probably came out of her mouth. As you can hear I'm not dead in a ditch or being kidnapped by aliens."

"I'm looking up flights right now," his voice sounded hollow, he'd put her on speaker.

"No, Dustin, you don't need to do that. I'm fine. It's been therapeutic doing this…it's going to sound weird, but…I think things are going to be okay now."

"Yeah?"

"Yeah…for some reason I feel really good, thank you."

"For what?"

"For being you."

"I do what I can," he said as the sound of his car starting up could be heard on Charlotte's end, "but I'm serious, I'll be on the next plane if you need me to be."

"I know," Charlotte could see the strip in the distance, "I need to get off the phone I've got to start paying attention to signs. I'll talk to you in a little while, okay?"

Hanging up the phone, she put her blinker on and drifted into the left lane, speeding up a bit. Downtown Las Vegas came into view, but it wasn't until she passed the Stratosphere that she recognized where she was. She had only been to Las Vegas once for a Bachelorette party, so she was only really familiar with the Strip itself and a few of the malls. From her car there was a dirty quality to Vegas in the daylight. It seemed like a completely different place without the sparkling lights to draw people into losing themselves in the dark. All the casinos lining the strip felt unrelated to other, like different puzzles pieces being forced to fit together in the same picture. A pyramid, okay we're in the desert, but a mini New York City skyline, a castle, a Colosseum, and an Eifel tower? Then there were the giant metal horse and ram sculptures as she was driving underneath the Russell Rd. underpass. They looked like they were in mid-gallop, whatever the hell that was about she wasn't sure.

From the signs, Charlotte knew she wasn't far from her destination. She got in the lane to follow I-215's entrance. Just exits away from meeting her birth mother, her nerves were beginning to put her on edge. A fast approaching sign said the Warm Springs Rd. exit was only a half a mile away. Cutting over to the exit lane, she coasted off the freeway, throwing her blinker on to turn left. There was an extra line in the address, Legacy #246, so Charlotte was keeping an eye out for apartment complexes of the same name.

Sitting at the next light she only saw shopping centers and gas stations, but leaning forward nearly pressing her nose against the windshield, she thought could see an apartment complex in the distance. Twisting in her seat she tried to find an address number on one of the four corners of the intersection to see where the even and odd numbers were.

No luck.

Then she saw the sign hanging on the traffic light across from her, S Eastern Ave 7300. Turning right on Eastern, she tried to see the numbers on the passing businesses, underneath one of the fast food signs nearest to the road on her right said 7355, so the evens were on the other side. With that in mind, she kept an eye out for the apartments on her left. As Charlotte was driving past the first complex she saw the numbers were too low. Driving on, hoping the upcoming apartments on the right could on the off chance be her destination because there was just a park on the left.

A red light had her stopped at Eastern and Robindale. Charlotte saw the Eastern 7700 sign hanging under the traffic light. Glancing at the handwritten address on the seat next to her she confirmed that was the correct address number for the apartment, but there wasn't a complex on any of the four corners. Had she gone too far? Had Ava written the address wrong? Confused, she made a right on Robindale to turn into the first housing development she came to. Pulling over to park, she grabbed at the road atlas. Charlotte studied the address and its coinciding place on the map; Ava's handwriting was legible, nothing like her own slanted print that ran together making everything look like a run-on doctor's signature. And Ava, as dramatic as she might be, wasn't the kind of person to make mistakes. The number existed, she must have passed it.

Tossing the map book back on the seat next to her, Charlotte threw the car in drive and made her way back down

Eastern the way she came. There could be two apartment complexes where she saw the first one; the second entrance she had dismissed could have been for an entirely different complex. As she drove she idly noticed there was a turn-in coming up with a sign marking the entrance. Squinting to read it, *seven-six-zero-zero.*

Charlotte's eyes widened as she slammed on the brakes at the last minute to make the right turn into the entrance. An angry honk sounded behind her at her poor driving. Nervous laughter escaped her, grateful she hadn't caused an accident. Feeling triumphant having found the address, she continued down the entrance road. At the end there was another sign with arrows directing incoming traffic. When she got close enough to read the words, it was as if at once all the air left her lungs.

Blinking her eyes hard, she opened them again. The words hadn't changed. *Mortuary.* She opened her car door and stepped out, the roads to the right and left lead to what she had thought was a sprawling park. Instead of basketball courts and swing sets, graves were in their place. She stared motionless at the sign.

"Ma'am, are you alright?"

Startled, Charlotte saw over the hood of her car an old man in a weathered pick-up truck.

"What?" Her voice weak, unsure if he meant her.

"Are you okay?" He enunciated.

How much time had passed? Her recognition was still

playing catch-up, "Yeah...I think..." her eyes drifted to the sign again and back to him, "I just didn't expect to find myself in a cemetery today."

His furrowed brow softened, sympathy clear in his eyes, "None of us ever do."

Charlotte feigned a smile.

"Take care now," he said, giving her a nod.

"You too..."

He steered his truck to the right and disappeared around the curve. Her car was still sitting in the middle of the road in the way of any traffic; she hadn't even heard him come up and pull around her car. Charlotte was lucky he'd been nice enough to check on her instead of yelling at her for being in the way. Then again, any visitor to a place like this wouldn't necessarily be in a road rage mood. To avoid inconveniencing anyone else, she got back in the car and decided to follow the path the pick-up had taken.

Coming around the first bend, she was surprised to see there weren't as many tombstones. Instead of the ones she'd seen in movies, there were flat markers in the ground. Row after row of markers stretched out across the lush green grass, coming so close to the road she could make out some of the names. Charlotte wasn't sure what she had expected and it dawned on her this was the first time she had ever been in a cemetery. Both of her windows were rolled down as she crept along, the silence filling her car. It was a mystery how being in middle of a city there could be so much quiet; it felt wrong disturbing it. The queasiness that she had thought abated was sending ripples of discomfort through her, as her grip on the steering wheel became increasingly clammy.

Fresh flowers seemed to be all over, almost at every grave. As she drove past she noticed engraved stones at the edges of the lawn closest to the road: *Sunrise*, *Mercy*, *Innocence*, he names of the areas of the cemetery. Charlotte's heart ached as she passed the *Innocence* area, all the teddy bears and pinwheels delicately placed amongst those graves. Poster-boards of picture collages reminding all who passed that not everyone got the chance to grow out of diapers. Toward the back of the cemetery was a woman with garden shears trimming around a marker in the ground, her hand brushing away the clippings. Just past her was another stone marking the next area that said *Legacy*. She was a car length away from the stone when her foot found the brake. Reaching for the road atlas, Charlotte confirmed what she was afraid of. Legacy was not the name of an apartment complex.

Not conscious of her actions, Charlotte found herself parked on the side of the road.

"Ava couldn't have known..." She mumbled to herself. Unless she had known and that's why she had offered to come with her, but Ava wouldn't leave her in the dark like that. She brushed the thought away.

There were more tombstone shaped markers in this area. Some were really elaborate, angels wrapping themselves around the deceased name, conjoined hearts for couples, many having only one of the hearts filled out, and a few had pictures embedded in their polished surfaces. Charlotte found her feet mere centimeters away from the grass. She hesitated to go further. Her unsettled stomach flipped. The last thing she wanted to do was throw up on someone's final resting place. Cringing at the notion, she noticed a small set of numbers on the marker closest to her. Checking the next closest stones she saw the numbers were increasing. She remembered the presumed apartment number and her feet began to move amongst the graves.

Charlotte came upon a modest granite stone. The matching numbers were on the back side, as she moved to face the slanted stone, her knees weakened in its presence. She gave in to kneeling, and moisture from the grass dampened her jeans, warming and cooling her at the same time. The name she'd imagined a face to her whole life was engraved in front of her. Trembling Charlotte reached out to touch it, unsure of what compelled her, and the moment her palm rested on the lukewarm stone she felt her calm reverie slip.

"I guess we weren't supposed to know each other..."

In her stupor, an orange mass caught her eye and she realized there was a vase nestled in the right side of the stone. The orange belonged to bloomed lilies in a bouquet. Peach roses accented them with Lantanas filling in the gaps, their yellow, coral, and pink colors standing out against the surrounding flowers. Brushing the edges of the petals with her finger tips, her nose picked up on their scent without even having to lean in. They were fresh. Charlotte hadn't seen anyone in the vicinity as she walked here, but someone must have visited her earlier today. The stone had the most simple of information, name, birth and death dates. There was no "In loving memory" or any indication of who buried her, just a gorgeous bouquet.

"Someone loves you…" A relieved smiled found its way onto her face, "I'm glad…" she said, wringing her hands, "I worried about that."

A pang of guilt prodded at Charlotte, "I should have brought flowers…How could I have known, right? I came here expecting…well, actually I don't know what I expected…I hadn't thought that far ahead. You were pretty young when you had me," Charlotte stared at the stone's engraved birth date, "I don't blame you, maybe you didn't have a choice…and even if you did…well, that's okay…I turned out fine. I got lucky."

She shifted to sit cross legged, "You're probably wondering why I came since I'm not searching for a mother I never had. I have a mom, I don't need another one."

Charlotte plucked a blade of grass, rubbing it between her fingers, "After what happened yesterday…I – I came to you because I need to know if the decision you made is the one I need to make."

***

With a last caress of the gravestone she could feel the warmth travel from the stone to her cool hands, the granite smooth under the pads of her fingers. Remnants of her earlier tears found their way to the corners of her eyes as she walked away. She would come back with flowers before she left tomorrow. It was the only way she could think to repay her, this fragmented woman she had tried to piece together her whole life.

Pulling her phone out Charlotte switched airplane mode back off and scrolled through her contacts. Tapping on the dial icon she moved the speaker to her ear, the artificial ringing echoing as she walked back to her car. Her nerves were no longer sending her stomach into a tumbling nauseous tornado.

"Hey mom…"

"Yeah, you know better than to listen to Ava."

"Mom, you wouldn't happen to be sitting down would you?"

"Really, I'm fine…"

"I just wanted to tell you…" a content smile emerging, "You're going to be a grandmother."

The Search for the Snow Tribe

By Noëlle de Beaufort

November 1784, Sierra Nevada Mountains

I will not freeze to death when I am so close. I will not die today.

Jean-Louis Chevalier reined in his horse and waited for the pack mules and spare horse to stop. He brushed the snow from his brow with a blood-stained deerskin glove, tattered and ripped from his journey. Snow-fog obscured the terrain. A fierce wind swirled around his exhausted limbs as he gathered his remaining strength to find shelter while the fading afternoon sunlight still remained.

Years as a trapper in Canada's far northern wilds had hardened him to winter's relentless assaults. He didn't merely survive life in frigid forests and on arctic tundra, he thrived on the adrenaline surge. Yet, inured as he was to the long season of biting ice, Jean-Louis was not accustomed to the high elevation of this wild Paiute mountain territory the Spanish called Sierra Nevada. His deliberate, deep gasps of cold air dissipated into shallow breaths. Finding shelter was urgent before he lost consciousness. Through a break in the fog, he glimpsed a pine grove not far ahead abutting a hill. *It can shelter us.*

He steeled himself to endure the pain in his near-frozen feet, gently pulled on the reins of the pack line, and forged toward the pines. A flash of movement captured his attention – a snowshoe hare mere yards away jumped up and then through a cache of pine boughs. Guessing the withered boughs had been cut by a man to hide a shelter, Jean-Louis dismounted. He winced in pain as his limbs, depleted of strength, hit the ground, but he forced himself forward, pushed the dead boughs aside and peered within. To his relief, the man-made cave was large enough for him, the horses and mules. He pulled them into the cave, took an axe from one of the mule packs, a cooking pot from another, and left the shelter to gather wood and snow. Back inside with a pot filled with snow-pack, and an armful of kindling and thick, hacked off branches, he set them down. After replacing the wind-breaking boughs over the cave entrance, he collapsed in exhaustion on the rock-strewn dirt. He closed his eyes for a moment, but he immediately rolled up onto his knees, knowing he could not afford to sleep in this biting cold. Game was about and he had found shelter to outlast the storm. *Tomorrow I will hunt and continue on my quest to find the Snow Tribe.*

His eyes adjusted to the darkness. He found a fire pit near the front of the cave, its ashes long dead. Opening his fire pouch, he removed flint and char cloth, unsheathed his hunting knife and began to strike the flint. When the char cloth began to glow, he transferred it to the tinder. Sparks finally flew and he blew on his creation. Jean-Louis began the process of unpacking the mules and unsaddling the horses, rubbing them down as he moved from the one to the next. He attached their feedbags, first watering them with snow-melt, then filling them with hay from the panniers. Once his companions were settled, he walked back to the fire, reached into his food pouch and removed pemmican and dried berries. *Not too much. I know not what lies ahead.*

The fire illuminated the cave, revealing wall drawings: wild horses, snowshoe hares, long-horned sheep, pronghorn, mountain goats, cougars and hunters like Jean-Louis, men with bows and arrows, stalking their game. To amuse himself, the French trapper imagined drawing his life on an empty part of the cave wall. *Perhaps one day I will come back to this cave and record my quest for posterity. Perhaps. But first I must complete it.*

Sated as much as he dared, Jean-Louis opened the flap of a special pocket sewn inside his cloak of silver fox pelts and pulled out a folded piece of leather. One side depicted a map of rivers from Canada to the Sierra Nevada; the other side showed detailed landmarks leading to a mountain village.

This map, drawn by a dying man, his friend, *Bagootsoo Atsa* of the Snow Tribe, had led him to this place.

The high-pitched whistling sound of the wind outside the cave reminded Jean-Louis of his first encounter with the Paiute a few months earlier.

August 1784, Saskatchewan River Crossing, Province of Alberta

Kneeling in darkness amongst tall prairie stalks, Jean-Louis swayed in sync with winds that rippled the surface of a grassy sea. Movement kept his muscles ready, helping him blend with nature's breath and avoid spooking any animal. With his bow held loosely at a forty-five degree angle, his arrow nocked, he waited. He meant to eat his prey, so he had left his flesh-tearing musket with his horse, tied up at an outcropping of trees half a mile away. The pale light of dawn broke over the horizon of the gently sloping terrain just as the antlers of a pronghorn, the fastest animal in North America, appeared. Estimating its speed, Jean-Louis raised his bow and prepared to loose an arrow from his hidden position when a piercing whistle startled both him and the buck, which bolted beyond his weapon's reach. The moment lost, Jean-Louis turned toward the sound, ready to curse the offending bird, but saw none. The whoosh of an arrow on his right alerted him to dive left. The cry of a wounded animal split the air. The steady rhythm of a man's feet crushed through the high grass. He looked up and stared into the black eyes of a red-and-black-streaked face. The Indian's hair was painted in the same colors.

Jean-Louis had cheated death many times since departing France for Québec a few years earlier, craving adventure on his own terms. He considered himself a man of destiny, invincible. He believed he could sense death's footsteps. Now, before the completion of his twenty-fourth year, fear flashed through him. *But if he meant to kill me, I'd be dead.*

Although the man standing over Jean-Louis spoke an unrecognizable language, his gestures were unmistakable.

Springing to his feet, Jean-Louis trained his vision in the direction of the man's pointed hand where a wounded cougar lay writhing on the ground, an arrow protruding from its gut. Following his deliverer's hand motion, Jean-Louis swept his bow from the ground, nocked the arrow again and aimed death's blow at the fallen predator.

The Indian nodded approval and brought his right fist to his chest.

Jean-Louis nodded back.

The Indian pointed to himself and said, "*Bagootsoo Atsa.*"

Jean-Louis pointed to himself and responded, "Jean-Louis." Following the pattern he established with his Indian scouts in Canada, he pointed to his rescuer. "*Ba-goot-soo-at-sa.*" The Frenchman was fluent in English and Spanish, passably conversant in German and several Canadian Indian languages, and prided himself on unerring inflection and mimicry.

His effort brought a smile to the Indian's face. "*Shan-loo-ee*," he said.

Jean-Louis nodded. "*Bien*. Good. *Français* or English?"

The Indian said, "No good parley."

Jean-Louis threw his head back and laughed. *An Indian who speaks English and French?*

The bare-chested native took rope hanging from the pronghorn skin belt that held up his buckskin apron, walked over to the big cat's limp body, yanked out the arrows, and pulled a large knife from a sheath on his belt.

Together they dressed the beast where it fell, discarding what could not be eaten or used. Jean-Louis expertly separated skin from carcass, set aside the protected pelt to dry while *Bagootsoo Atsa* turned his attention to the meat, proving himself a skillful butcher.

While his new friend methodically cut up the cougar, Jean-Louis went back to the nearby trees, intending to untie his horse and lead it back to the cougar to pack and carry the meat and pelt. When he reached the grove, he stopped in stunned silence. The Indian's horse was grazing next to his. *What kind of fool is this Indian? He knew not whether my horse belonged to friend or foe. Why did he protect me?*

Jean-Louis led both horses back to the kill site.

Each took empty bags from their saddle packs, filled

them with meat, and jointly flung the cougar's skin over the back of the trapper's horse.

Jean-Louis pointed to his horse, and said, "Pégase."

Bagootsoo Atsa pointed to his horse and said, "Dreaming Wind."

They led their horses back to the grove and unpacked the meat and lay it out in the sun to dry after treating it with salt, except for the portion they would eat now. Jean-Louis began to build a fire. The Paiute cut branches, stripped them of bark, and built a turning spit over the fire. Once the cougar thighs were affixed to the spit, the two new friends sat on the ground.

Jean-Louis raised his arms in question and said, "Why did you help me?"

The Indian said, again, "No good parley." In the dry dirt, he drew a man lying as if in death, pointed to his chest, and then drew a stick man, pointed to it and said, "*Shan-loo-ee.*"

"But I didn't kill you!" protested Jean-Louis.

"No kill. Sleep. Dream meet you."

"A dream?"

They drew, gestured, spoke and slowly began to understand each other. After awhile, the Indian drew a familiar animal.

"Buffalo!"

He smiled, pointed to himself and then the drawing and said, "*Bagootsoo! Bagootsoo!*"

"Your name means buffalo? *Buffle!*"

Bagootsoo Atsa reached into his quiver and picked out an arrow and pricked his finger. As the blood dripped, he said, "*At-sa.*"

"Blood?" asked Jean-Louis. "Buffalo Blood or Blood of the Buffalo?"

"No." The Indian pointed to the red stripe on his blanket, and a red mark on the boots Jean-Louis wore.

"Red! The color red!" said Jean-Louis. "Red Buffalo!"

The Indian nodded. As the meat roasted, he drew and haltingly told his story. He had been born under an unusual celestial conjunction of stars. To the tribe's shaman, *Ggwe'na'a Toha*, White Eagle, the sky signs foretold a seer of unusual power. The healer knew that such a visionary, a dreamer of truth with a gift for seeing "the beyond, came forth only once in a century. Believing that this special child embodied the tribe's destiny, he taught Red Buffalo the ways of a medicine man.

"Green Eyes, *Ebbooee Poohe,* father. White man. Speak English and French. White Eagle save from wolves when small. Mother, *Nibabi Mula*, Snow Moon, daughter of White Eagle." He drew two children. Pointing to himself, he said, "*Bagootsoo Atsa*," and to the other, *Taba Uweka Atsa*, Red Sunset.

The shaman of a tribe guarded and refined healing herbs and potions, dispensing them to members of the tribe to heal sickness, ease suffering or even hasten death, chanting ancient words passed down through the generations. The last of the Snow Tribe's stores of a magical plant that brought the near-dead back to life had been buried in an avalanche with half the village two winters past. Since then, death had visited too many too soon, and the White Eagle had directed Red Buffalo to travel north on a vision quest, to dream the location of the life-saving plant and bring it back to the tribe. White Eagle was too old to make the trek; only Red Buffalo could find its growing place, hidden to all but shamans.

So Red Buffalo had ventured north, dreaming each night of where he should search the next day. The dream of Jean-Louis had led him to this grassy plain.

"Why me?" asked Jean-Louis. "I know of no magical plants. I can be of no help to you."

Red Buffalo smiled, and said, "Not know why. Know must find you. Found you. Tonight dream again our journey."

"*Our* journey? I am far from anywhere I know. I have been following the night stars, trying to get back to a river or familiar landmark." While speaking, Jean-Louis drew stars and spirals. "I wanted a summer's adventure, to see the west, the wild buffalo." He sat in silence and surveyed the prairie until his eyes fixed on Red Buffalo. "Finding this plant would be an adventure. *Oui*, yes, I will accompany you."

For the next weeks, the two men traveled unmarked trails in the direction dreamed by Red Buffalo until they found the wildflower meadow where the magical plant grew, shielded by a waterfall. After they gathered enough roots, leaves, seeds and flowers, Red Buffalo stripped off his clothes and stood beneath the wall of water.

Dusty, sweaty and dirty from their trek, Jean-Louis joined him, and as they lay in the sun afterward, Jean-Louis said, "Your hair! The paint has washed off, but your hair is still red. Do you make dye from a special plant?"

"No paint. No dye. White man hair. Sister same. Her eyes green like father."

Jean-Louis' jaw dropped and he laughed. "You are wrapped in a web of mysteries, my friend."

"Mis-trr-ee? What this?"

"Something hidden that we have to discover, like the magical plant."

"But plant not hidden; plant reveal itself. Nothing hidden. What I need know, I see."

Their path back toward the mountains of the Snow Tribe followed the rivers, so they had ample water and fish to sustain them. Jean-Louis saved Red Buffalo from a black bear with a shot from his musket, and Red Buffalo saved Jean-Louis from a wolf attack with his tomahawk.

After weeks of travel, the days were noticeably shorter. One day they hid from a party of white men, and overheard them talking of a nearby trading post and small village. Once the men had passed, Jean-Louis and Red Buffalo tracked the men until they spied the village from a safe distance. Later that night, at their camp, Jean-Louis said, "We may need to obtain provisions to continue. I am thinking we might need a mule or two unless water, grass and game are plentiful in your mountains."

Red Buffalo nodded. "Night chills; snows come. Snow give water. Animals and birds hide; can find. Horses need grass."

"It's best if I go alone; we don't know how the villagers will react to seeing an Indian. To them, you could be either a willing trader or a hostile enemy. On the frontier, fear is more powerful than trust."

Red Buffalo nodded.

The next morning, Jean-Louis rode into town, purchased two mules and outfitted them with provisions. By late afternoon, he had rejoined Red Buffalo south of the trading post.

Just after they made camp for the night, the click of the cocking of a musket alerted Red Buffalo, who threw himself over Jean-Louis, just as the shot was fired, forcing him to the ground.

Pinned underneath Red Buffalo's bleeding body, Jean-Louis could see the boots of a lone man approaching.

"I knew you was probably some Injun-lovin' Frenchy," said a voice thick with whiskey, spitting out the slurred words. "You still alive, Frenchy? Or did I get both of you with one shot?" The sound of the cocking mechanism clicked again as the boots slowly advanced, while the voice kept on. "Goddam Injun's bleedin' so much, I can't tell."

Jean-Louis reached for the knife sheathed in his boot,

and with a practiced flick of the wrist, threw his blade into the creeping killer's heart.

When he was certain that the stillness hid no other assassins, Jean-Louis eased himself from under Red Buffalo's limp body to examine his friend's injury.

The bullet had pierced the Indian's spine. Blood spurted from the wound; his breathing was shallow and labored. Jean-Louis knew he could not remove the bullet without worsening the fatal wound. He attempted to slow the bleeding with pressure from his hand as he turned the Indian's body on its side.

His voice raspy, his eyes pleading, Red Buffalo whispered, "My friend, *Shan-Loo-ee*, finish journey back to Snow Tribe. Take medicine plant Snow Tribe. Follow deerskin map. *Shan-Loo-ee*, dreamed you take flower magic my people. Take amulet from neck. Give Red Sunset, she share heart. Forever." Red Buffalo grabbed his friend's forearm. "Dreaming Wind find village. Make haste. Snows come."

Jean-Louis said, "Yes, my friend. I will complete your quest."

Red Buffalo smiled, and closed his eyes. "Snow Tribe more important than one man. Last journey, go alone." His hand dropped.

Jean-Louis buried his friend under the moonlight, and broke camp to move away from the killer's body, a lone target to be ripped apart by the ravenous predators that roamed the forest.

When he finally stopped for the night, warmed by fire, the French trapper fell into a deep sleep.

November 1784

A sound awoke Jean-Louis as light dawned. It was not the wind, nor the sound of any bird he recognized. It was a human whistle. All he could do now was hope he had followed the map correctly and that Red Buffalo's amulet would identify him as a friend of the Snow Tribe. He whispered the words Red Buffalo had taught him, "*Ggwe'na'a Toha*," over and over, a chant of divine protection to save him if confronted by hostile captors. Whether it would work or not, he did not know. He had not mastered the cool courage of Red Buffalo, who feared nothing because as a seer, he knew all that would happen. That last day he had known that death awaited, yet followed his destiny to the end.

Jean-Louis could imagine all manner of unpleasant outcomes, but to know for sure the moment he would die, that knowledge he did not desire. He believed there was always a chance to live.

Another whistle put him on edge. He realized that the cold had dulled his mental and physical prowess. He must guard his strength for what lay ahead. According to the map, he was close. He could not hide forever in this freezing jail. He crawled slowly to the front of the cave, and peered out.

Two braves were creeping near. The smoke of his fire, the trail of his footprints, the sound of the neighs of his horses, any and all would have signaled his presence in this unknown land of white peaks, white fog and white snow cover.

Taking a deep breath, he called out the name Red Buffalo had taught him, "*Ggwe'na'a Toha!* White Eagle! *Ggwe'na'a Toha!*"

The men stopped in their tracks, readied their arrows and one called back words that Jean-Louis did not recognize.

He called out the other words Red Buffalo had taught him, "*Hainch Ki-tum-ar-g*," which roughly was "Hello," but closer to "Friend, talk it out." Then he repeated the name of the medicine man, "*Ggwe'na'a Toha!*"

The braves repeated, "*Hainch Ki-tum-ar-g*," lowered their bows, but kept their bowstrings taut.

Jean-Louis grabbed his pouch and weapons, pushed the boughs aside, and emerged from the cave's mouth.

They motioned to Jean-Louis to come forward.

The younger Paiute circled behind the Frenchman, poking him in various places, grunting unintelligible words to his companion, who had two snowshoe hares slung over his shoulder on a rope. He pushed Jean-Louis forward.

Jean-Louis gestured toward the cave, trying to convey that his horses and mules were in the cave, so the younger Indian went to look and brought out the animals and other items after he had extinguished the fire. The elder Paiute led Jean-Louis and the pack line of horse and mules; the younger Indian trailed behind. They trudged through the snow for what seemed like several miles until the sun reached the sky's midpoint, the first clear day the French trapper had seen in more than a week.

They approached a small village of *wicki-ups;* it looked just as Red Buffalo had described. The dome-like structures, made of branches and grass, were now hidden beneath snow, which served as both insulation and camouflage. Stumbling over an unseen buried boulder, Jean-Louis tumbled head first into a blanket of white powder. The braves laughed and hauled him up. They nudged his shoulders forward and escorted him into the village.

The elders emerged to greet the stranger. *Red Buffalo saved me a third time by teaching me the name of the medicine man.* He said the name again, with the inflection of a question, "*Ggwe'na'a Toha*?"

A diminutive man with a cape of black-tipped fox fur pelts and headdress of black and white feathers stepped forward, pointed to his chest and said, "*Ggwe'na'a Toha.*"

The emphasis on one syllable was different than Jean-Louis had said, so he repeated the name as its owner pronounced it. Pointing to himself, he said, "Jean-Louis. *Hainch Ki-tum-ar-g, Ba-goot-soo At-sa.* "

At the mention of Red Buffalo's name, whispers filled the cold air.

The medicine man knew some English. "*Shan-loo-ee,* where *Ba-goot-soo At-sa*?"

The French trapper said, "*Mort.* Dead. I have medicine plant and seeds and gift for *Ta-ba At-sa.*" He remembered the word for "sun," which was "*Ta-ba*," but not the word for "sunset," so he hoped that Red Sun would bring forth the sister of his fallen friend. He retrieved the dried flowers, leaves, roots and seeds from his pouch as well as the leather map drawn by Red Buffalo. "'*Snow Tribe more important than one man.*' This was said by *Ba-goot-soo At-sa.*"

The medicine man stepped forward."*Ba-goot-soo At-sa* save many with gift. May Great Spirit protect him on final journey.*"

Whispers echoed from the tribe as a woman stepped forward. She had red hair and green eyes.

"*Ta-ba At-sa*?"

"*Ta-ba U-we-ka At-sa.*"

Jean-Louis recognized the name, and repeated, "*Ta-ba U-we-ka At-sa.*" He lifted a leather strap from around his neck and over his head. An amulet dangled from the cord.

Ta-ba U-we-ka At-sa gasped.

The French trapper extended his hand to her and said, "From *Ba-goot-soo At-sa* . His heart will be with you always."

Red Sunset's clear green eyes misted with tears that fell unbidden down her cheeks. She stepped forward and accepted the gift from her brother, raising the cord over her head to let it fall from her neck over her white-dyed leather tunic. Holding it to her heart, she lowered her head in silent thanks.

The medicine man said, "Come, Guest. Eat. Drink. Sleep."

Jean-Louis was gathered up in arms from every angle and half-carried to the campfire, where game was roasting.

After a dinner of mountain goat and dried berries, Jean-Louis joined the elders in the chief's *wicki-up* and told the tale of his adventures with Red Buffalo. He re-enacted following the trail dreamed by Red Buffalo that led to the meadow where the healing flowers were veiled by the waterfall, being ambushed multiple times by wild animals and, finally, encountering the assassin.

Jean-Louis looked around the small council and sensed their understanding. "It took many days and nights to reach you. Tomorrow I must leave for home before winter's full fury is unleashed."

White Eagle spoke. "Too late now, *Shan-Loo-ee*. Snows come. You must stay until the rivers run again. You will hunt with us. You will teach us white man ways. Then you return to *Can-a-da*."

Jean-Louis sat in silence. *At this altitude, unclear trails, ice storms, and unknown predators await me. The trek is months long. I have no choice.* He nodded agreement.

The elders offered Jean-Louis more of a berry drink and they told stories of Red Buffalo until long into the night.

The shaman led Jean-Louis back to his *wicki-up,* and said, "I make bed for you. Wait."

Standing under the moonlight, jean-Louis heard footsteps and turned to see Red Sunset.

She gazed directly into the French trapper's blue eyes; her fingers twirled the amulet. "Brother born with me. Same night under same stars. Each night, we dream same dreams. You will leave when waters flow, *Shan-loo-ee*. But you will return. I have dreamed it. We are old in dream. We die together."

Jean-Louis smiled. A new adventure had begun.

The Old White Dude's Note

By John Hill

Me and LaTeisha, she's my best friend, we was on our bikes about 10:30 that night when we saw the old white dude climb out of Mizz Duncan's house across the street, jackin' her TV.

We started giggling and shit, watchin' this old white guy strugglin' out the window with this big-ass TV. Guys stealin' stuff, usually brothers, they young, fast, just shadows. But here's this old huffin' and puffin' white dude struggling now to carry the TV away, at night, nobody around but us. We supposed to be doin' our 7th grade homework then go to bed. Mama's a nurse, works nights, trusts me, so I sneak out with LaTeisha, her mama's drinks, don't know shit after dinner, we just ride our bikes around. The old guy saw us, must have figured we just girls on bikes, ain't no thang. He wrong.

"Check it out, girl," LaTeisha said, "get us a cell phone, film his ass, put it on YouTube, got ourselves the world's oldest burglar!"

"Damn, girl," I said, grinning. "Ain't no rush. Snail just passed his ass."

We giggled. He finally had to set the TV down, at Mizz Duncan's curb, then, he turned, sat down on it, exhausted. Looked like he might die there.

We peddled across the street, getting around thirty feet away, ridin' in figure 8's in the street.

"Hey, you girls!" the old man suddenly said, panting. "You want to earn five dollars?"

We stopped peddling, kept our distance.

"Find me a shopping cart or a wagon, I'm parked two blocks away, and I just bought this TV and --"

But we started laughin', pointin', got him looking all around fast.

"Man, you didn't buy shit!" I yelled. "We saw you jackin' Mizz Duncan's TV!"

"She in the hospital, she older'n dirt, house all empty," LaTeisha added, "we just saw you carryin' that out! How 'bout you give us fifty bucks, we don't start screamin' and shit? Get your wrinkly-old white ass in jail, huh?"

"Teisha!" I exclaimed, hit her on the arm. Don't need her gettin' me in any more trouble with my Mama, after last week and cigarettes. Teisha shrugged, hit me back on the other arm, not hard.

"No, no, please, don't yell," he said, quiet-like, reached into his big jacket, pulls out two gray candleholder things, size

42

of a Bud Lite.

"I don't have fifty dollars, but here, you each take one of these, sterling silver."

LaTeisha and I didn't know what to do, this gettin' all weird-ass now. Car drove by, slowed, drove on.

"You the world's oldest burglar, or some shit?" I asked, doin' my tough.

"You tell us what's goin' on, we maybe turn you in, we maybe don't," Teisha said, "and do it fast, old man, cause we can scream at your ass anytime."

"No, please," he said, setting the candlestick holders down, still tired. "I just need to catch my breath. Just go away, leave me alone..."

We say no. So he takes out a small folded note from his jacket pocket, started to put it inside his shirt pocket.

"What's that note?" I asked. "And you tell the truth now, or I be screamin' and I can make every porch light on the block come on, brothers come runnin' with ball bats, save poor me and Teisha from this old white guy, comin' at us --"

Teisha giggled, especially when the old man got his ass all agitated and shit.

"No! Please! Just go away!"

"YOU TELL US WHY YOU JACKIN' MRS. DUNCAN'S HOUSE, OLD MAN," Teisha said, really, really loud.

"YEAH, WHAT YOU BE DOIN' IN OUR 'HOOD, WHAT'S THAT NOTE, WHY--"

"Okay, okay, please, be quiet," he said, scared,

looking around.

We got quiet. A porchlight came on two houses down. Might have been Mr. Cavendish's house. I pointed at it and said in a quiet voice, "Better be the damn truth or they gonna bust your ass fast."

"All right, okay..." he said, then pointed to the house. "I grew up in that house. My parents were always mean to me. When I was seven, one night, I heard them arguing, I heard for the first time, I was adopted. And they were sayin' they were sorry now, I was too much trouble, cost too much money, they didn't know what to do now, how they were stuck with me." The old dude's voice kind of changed now.

Teisha and I got quiet.

"I went to my room and cried. I knew adopted meant I had a real mother somewhere and at seven, I just knew she'd loved me and was looking for me. So I wrote a note to her, saying 'Mama, my real mama, I love you now I know you're gonna come get me and we'll be happy. I love you, your son, Frank.' I wanted there to be, I don't know, a record, a message, somewhere in the world, while I waited, in case I died or something, I don't know, I was just seven. I snuck up in the attic, wedged the note in some boards, out of sight. Well, my real Mama never came, and I grew up and we all moved away, and I lived my life, but my heart ain't so good now, so I kept wondering if I dreamed it, and that note's proof of how I felt, what happened..."

Teisha started twirlin' her hair a little. She does that,

she's payin' real attention.

"Started thinkin' about it, more and more, for years," he say. "I live over a thousand miles away, Portland, Oregon, not easy gettin' back here. Had me an old Chevvy but it played out after 200 miles. I started to take a Greyhound back to Portland, but I ain't got much going on there, no big deals, or family, so I realized, with this bum ticker, I ain't gonna live forever, so I had to do this. So I hitchiked. Who picks up an old man hitchhiking? Only truck drivers, but a few gave me a lift. I got let off near a railroad yard, trains heading the way I was heading. Hell, I ain't hopped a freight train since back in '57, so it scared me. Get your legs cut off easy, tryin' to run alongside them train cars. But I was low on cash and I felt like I was on a mission, on some crazy quest, to get back here to Nevada, see if that note was still here. It had gotten important to me, I knew it didn't make much sense. So I go down and hide in the shadows near the freight cars and --"

Just then, Mr. Cavendish, he big, fat, and black, and always talked like white people, wore some sweater too, he walked up to us from down the street.

"Are you girls okay?" he asked us. And he stared at the old white dude.

Me and Teisha, we looked at each other. Good time to bust this old white guy, and his long-ass story, but I didn't feel like it. Teisha didn't either.

"We okay," Teisha said.

"What's going on here?" Mr. Cavendish asked, glaring

at the old white dude.

"Well, Mizz Duncan," I say, quick, "she had some men help her set this old TV out by the curb for the trash guys to take. This old guy, he was askin' us if we thought it was okay for him to maybe take."

Teisha looked at me, impressed. I can lie fast as I can talk.

"That right?" Mr. Cavendish asked ol' Frank, who nodded, waved, like, yes.

"He bring his car back later, get this TV," Teisha say, twirling her hair. "We say, it's okay, Miz Duncan didn't want it no more."

Mr. Cavendish thought it over a few moments, then turned and as he walked away, said, "You young ladies need to be home. Too late out for you to be riding around on your bicycles, talking to strangers. A word to the wise is sufficient."

We said okay, and we three were quiet as Mr. Cavendish walked away far enough that he couldn't hear us anymore. We looked at old Frank, who was all nervous and shit now.

"Girls, really, just a wagon or maybe a shopping cart, so I can get this TV and get out of here, okay? Take the candlesticks, here, then --"

"Nah, you finish your story," I said. "You jump on a train to get here?"

"And what's a quest?" Teisha added.

"Yes, I jumped aboard a freight train to get here, don't

make much sense, I know that," old Frank say, gesturing. "When I was getting off it, outside Las Vegas here, two men jumped me. Took the last of my cash, hurt my rib, smashed my nose, it was all bloody. I was lying there in a ditch, thinking, this is a really good time to forget about all this and just try to get home."

We waited. I hoped Mr. Cavendish didn't come back. I hate not knowin' the end of a story.

"But I had to know before I got too old," old Frank said, "before I died. Was it all something a 7 year old saw on TV, about adoption, or was it real, when I was a boy? Did my real Mama come? Did someone find my note, move it? So finally got back to this neighborhood, twenty minutes ago, my old home where I rode a bicycle around this same street, like you girls do now."

"This all for some note?" Teisha asked.

"I broke in, to see if that note was still there, and it was," he held it up, smiled. "It's my note to my real mother, that I never did ever meet or anything." He looked down. "But I tried. That little boy, 70 years ago, tried...to reach out...I was saying, I was here, I felt things. It was real, it happened. Don't know why that matters to me now, but..." He shrugged, smiled.

We all three quiet. Then I said something I didn't mean.

"Bullshit, you just jackin' some TV and candlesticks."

"No, you can read it," old Frank say, givin' me the yellowy old folded-up note. "And I just took the TV and the candlesticks on the way out, because, why not?"

He suddenly grinned his bad teeth, shrugged. Teisha and I giggled. Why not?

But then, all quiet and shit, Five-O rolled up on us. Siren burped, red and blue spinnin' cop lights, went down fast. Old Frank, he tries to run for it, pantin', old arms flailin' around, cops jump out, run, catch him, haul him over to the squad car, but now he's gaspin', grabbin his chest, face and sounds like a baby cryin', paramedics run up, porch lights goin' on, people in the streets, then ol' Frank, his arm slumps down, not moving. Starin' off, not seein'. They check him, put him in the ambulance. They turned off the lights and sirens when they drove him away, regular speed.

I hid my candlestick under my mattress. I think I can sell it to my friend Janine's older brother, he got a garage full of DVD players, still in the boxes. Buy cigarettes.

And I read Frank's note. Shaky little kid writing, old crinkly paper, sayin' what he said. I hid the note inside a plaster crack in my closet, no one would find it, ever. Seems to me, little boy's note to his mother, sayin' I love you, come get me? Long as that note's there, it be like he loves her, she loves him, only they can't find each other, not yet. I ain't gonna be the one throw that note away.

Last year, I finally stopped mailin' off Christmas cards to the Daddy I don't know. This year, I think I'll send him a card again, tell him I'm here. I ain't gonna tell him I love him, I don't know him, but I'm here, waitin' to. Maybe he write back.

Rescue or Recovery?

By Marshall Prescott

Chris wiped the sweat from his brow as he thought about his dad. He had to talk with the search team about where to look for him. This was not it, he was sure of that. But what could he say that would make them listen to him, after all they were the professionals.

A searcher stopped within a few feet of Chris to catch his breath.

"Kinda tough terrain up here, don't you think?" He said to Chris in an attempt to be friendly.

"Yeah, I've been working up quite a sweat. How've you been doing?

The young man swabbed his face and neck with his handkerchief and put his cap back on before answering. "This would go a little bit better if it wasn't so hot up here. This is probably the worst time of the year to be combing through the countryside. But once the sun gets behind Mount Charleston it's gonna cool down a little, maybe even ten to fifteen degrees."

"Yeah" Chris said brushing more sweat from his face with his open hand. "That's why we've got to find Dad soon. He might not have had any water with him when he went down. Dad was pretty fussy about his survival package, but you know how it is with water in this kind of heat." His voice trailed off as he was looking down the ravine they were standing next too.

"Okay, I better keep moving. It's easier to cover more ground that way," the searcher smiled.

Chris nodded without saying anything.

The searcher was happy to be moving on. He didn't know what he could say to Chris. It's tough losing someone in a plane crash. But when it's your old man and you're only sixteen years old, it's probably a lot more difficult.

Chris began walking up the mountainside again looking for some larger areas that could harbor a small aircraft. He didn't know what to do. He knew this wasn't the right place. He felt it was wrong, but no-one wanted to listen to him yesterday when he told them. Even his older brother, Jake blew him off when Chris spoke up. Jake was betting on the professionals with their fancy college degrees saying: this is the area where he was flying; this is where he would have gone down, and this was where they would look for the crash.

Chris was not sure of himself yet either, and that made

it worse for him. He was young, and had to admit it didn't help when he got angry discussing things with the others last night. Now they wouldn't listen to him at all. The only reason he was up here looking in this area was he didn't have the gear he needed to go to where he thought they should be searching. That and he hadn't been able to convince anyone else to go there either.

"What does he know? He's just a kid." One of them said at last night's meeting. They were convinced that his age kept Chris from knowing anything.

With the sun beating down on them relentlessly, progress was slow. Everyone up on the mountain, except Chris, was an experienced search and rescue person was trained to handle this steep terrain without getting hurt or killed trying to find an aircraft. Even Jake had experience in environments like this one. He had been in the Iraq war. He had existed in hot weather and mountainous terrain.

The second night of searching they still had not located him. Chris began to think of happier times with his father. He and his dad had flown over this mountain many times. Dad liked the other side better. There were more ravens and more wild life on the other side too. Suddenly another thought made Chris stop dead in his tracks. Perhaps his father had survived the crash impact and if he was in a shaded area where the sun wasn't beating down on him, dehydrating him, perhaps he may be waiting for the search party to rescue him. Then the knot in his stomach brought his attention back to where he was again.

How could he convince the rescue workers where they should be looking for his father? What could he say to his brother that would convince him to join him in searching the other side?

Just then Chris' left foot slipped and gave way, sending him falling backwards smashing his shoulder into a small cactus just missing the side of his face. He rolled over and got back up before anyone could spot him on the ground. He didn't want anyone to think he wasn't able to handle the terrain. The cactus quills in his shoulder stung and hurt with each movement he made, but he couldn't stop searching. He would let someone remove them after the search was completed for the day.

Another thought struck Chris. He would have one more discussion with his brother about where to search. He would have to approach him tonight subtlety after everyone had eaten dinner, before the meeting. If he could convince Jake first then there was a chance, although a small one, but certainly a chance that the search party would listen to where they should be searching.

Darkness fell as they were being transported back to camp headquarters. No one was saying much around Chris. Perhaps they just didn't know what to say to the boy. Everyone was hot, thirsty, and hungry as well. They would eat and re-hydrate before discussing what quadrant to search tomorrow.

Dinner came and went. The knot in his stomach grew

bigger; feeling like a horse had kicked him in the mid-section. One of the supervisors glanced at his wounded shoulder and commented to him.

"You need to get that looked at son. If that gets infected, you'd be excluded from searching tomorrow. The medic can probably take care of that for you."

"Thanks. I'll go see her. But first, I need to speak with my brother before we regroup for the meeting."

"Okay, but the longer you wait Chris the more time it has to get infected."

"Yeah, okay. I'm done eating anyway. I gotta speak with Jake first. Okay? Then I'll go right afterwards." He pushed himself away from the table and stood.

It only took minutes for him to find Jake talking with another rescuer next to the latrines.

"Can we talk for a minute, Jake?"

"Sure. What's up?" The other searcher took the hint.

"Well I, ah…. I'd like to have your support at the meeting tonight when I bring up searching the other side of the mountain."

"Not again Chris. We discussed this last night, and I told you we would follow what the professionals recommended. They do this stuff all the time and they determined that we are on the right side of the mountain now." Jake said. "I can't believe you're bringing this up again."

"I know those guys are the professionals at the search stuff, but I flew with Dad millions of times and he liked flying the other side of the mountain. I think we're wasting our time on this side. We need to switch to the other side." Chris pleaded.

"Need I remind you that I am in charge of the business when Dad is not here, and I say we follow the search and rescue team?" Jake said clenching his jaw.

"I'm not arguing about who is running the business, I'm telling you that Dad used to fly on the other side of the mountain, and that's where we should be searching." Chris demanded. "You think that because I'm younger, I can't be right. But I flew more with Dad than you did, and he liked to fly on the other side of the mountain."

"Okay, look. We're getting nowhere on this. I'll tell you what, we'll bring up the subject at the meeting, and see what they say. Okay?"

"Okay. Finally." Chris said with a smile.

"Don't get too confident just yet. Remember they didn't like the idea yesterday. But we'll see what they think of it tonight." Jake said feeling better about the issue now that Chris was smiling.

Chris was excited now. Finally his brother was on his side. He could hardly wait for the meeting now.

He went to the medic station and let her look at his wound. She removed a couple of quills and flushed the area with saline solution several times, then applied a bandage to keep it clean. "You were fortunate. It looks like most of the quills went straight through. I flushed out the sand and dirt as best as I could. And I applied a bandage to keep it clean for you."

Chris thanked her and headed to the tent for the organizational meeting that was about to begin.

One of the team leaders whistled and everyone began to assemble for the meeting. Chris eagerly took a chair waiting for the discussion to begin.

The Captain walked to the front of the tent clearing his throat and pushing his hat back on his head. "Alright, everyone sit down and rest your weary body while I go over a couple things. First, thanks to all of you for coming out here and assisting with this search. His family is represented here with both sons' assisting our efforts too.

"Second, we have finished covering the first three grids. That's a major accomplishment in this heat. This mountain can be relentless when it comes to the weather up here and we all know how difficult it gets. Not to mention, determining where to search."

Walking over to the edge of the tent he held up a bottle of water. "Make sure you're all re-hydrating too. We're already looking for one man; we don't want to have to airlift one of you out of here too."

As the Captain continued to discuss the search quadrant for the following day, Chris's attention faded. He was thinking of his father waiting for help to arrive. Trying to survive the elements, rationing his water supply and food he had on board the aircraft. He may be busted up badly and not able to rig up a makeshift shelter. The not knowing was killing Chris. He just didn't do well, when uncertainty was a factor in things, and when it came to his father. He was the best man on earth as far as Chris was concerned, and no-one could measure up to him.

Something jarred Chris back to reality. They were discussing the issue of searching the other side of Mount Charleston. Jake was speaking now, but didn't sound very convincing. "We wanted to bring up the subject of searching the other side of the mountain again. "My brother and I think there is merit to my father flying on the opposite side. I know we discussed it a little bit last night, but we wanted to revisit the issue."

As Jake talked there was some grumbling from some of the guys in the back. They weren't too keen on searching anywhere the Captain didn't specify. A couple of the guys got up and got more water during the discussion.

The Captain put his hands up to quiet the group so he could speak. "Yes, I know, we discussed this issue last night. I'd have to say, and I agree with the others here, that the flight plan that was filed showed his flight on this side of the mountain, not the other side, Jake."

Jake shot a look at Chris as if to say he tried to convince them but to no avail.

Chris got up from his chair and forcefully pushed his chair back to its original position. It collapsed with a banging noise as he exited the tent. Jake followed after his younger brother.

Jake waited until he was out of ear shot of the team before calling after his brother, "Chris wait up. I want to talk to you. Please?"

Chris didn't look back or respond. He kept walking. *The further I get from these people the better I'll like it right now. How could they call themselves rescuers? They didn't want to rescue anyone. They just want to be in control of where they searched regardless of where my father is right now.*

Jake began running in order to catch up to his brother. Breathing heavy as he reached Chris he said, "Wait, you knew this was going to happen. You knew they wouldn't like your idea. They didn't like it yesterday either, remember?"

"Nobody gives a damn, so why should I say anything?" Chris said without looking at Jake.

Chris kicked a small rock with his foot and then turned towards Jake with a scowl on his face. "Just because I'm a kid, no one thinks I know anything. No one thinks that I may know anything about what I say because I'm young. Screw them. I don't have time to listen to those idiots. Dad's life is on the line."

"I tried Chris. They just don't feel that Dad was on the other side of the mountain, that's all. It doesn't have anything to do with your age," Jake lied.

Chris picked up a stone and threw it as hard as he could. Then looked at Jake and said, "They don't want to search the other side. Why?"

"They said he was flying on this side. That's why we're searching on this side, dude. The aviation board at the airport said radar indicated he was on this side. That's why we're on this side searching," Jake said shaking his hands to emphasize his words.

Chris picked up another stone and heaved it into the canyon. He was still frustrated and angry. He knew they should be searching the other side, where his father flew all the time.

"Okay, Jake. You win. Chris was tired of talking when nothing changed. "I'm going to turn in. I'm tired and need to get some sleep." Chris said as he walked toward the sleeping quarters.

"Okay. I have to finish talking with the Captain and then I'll join you."

I know I'm right. Now what can be done about it? Chris knew that every twenty-four hour period brought less hope that his father had survived the crash if he had survived at all. But Chris wouldn't consider that thought. He climbed into his bunk and tried to sleep. Just like the night before he only dosed off and on. No deep sleep came.

In the early morning hours, Chris got up before anyone else began to stir. He crept out of the sleeping quarters so quiet that no one woke up. It gave him time to get some ropes and supplies before anyone knew what he was doing. He was going to the other side of the mountain to look for his father.

He put several bottles of water, along with carabineer clips, spikes, a climbing hammer, granola bars, and miscellaneous stuff he thought might come in handy, stuffing it all into his backpack. Then he tied ropes onto his backpack and slipped into it. It was so heavy it almost toppled him over backwards at first. He struggled to get the backpack into position on his back before securing the straps.

He scribbled a note and set off on a trail he knew would get him on the other side before anyone could discover he was gone. He knew the first rule about search and rescue was never go alone, but he had to break that rule in order to find his father.

Chris was glad the moonlight was bright enough to illuminate his path. It made it a little easier for him to negotiate his steps allowing him to avoid the unstable hillside gravel. The area he wanted to search first was known as Robbers Roost. It was a treacherous area, and combing through it would be strenuous, but he recalled his father flying over it many times in their travels. So he wanted to search that area first.

When the sun began to peek over the horizon, Chris was almost to the top of the cliff overlooking Robbers Roost. He put on his climbing harness and threaded his safety rope through it. Before he descended he took one last look at the sunrise. Its orange glow washing over him as he said to no-one, "Well dad, here I come." With those words still on his lips he began his trek down the steepest side all the way down to the first ledge.

He hammered in another anchor, and clipped the rope as he looked around at the foliage below him. It was too dense to see much. His father could easily be in the wreckage down there and be impossible to see from this location. He was eager to descend to another shelf.

The radio came to life with them calling him, asking where he was located. He reached it with his other hand and turned the switch off and said, "Nothing is going to stop me from descending down there to find my father dead or alive." He preferred alive of course. But Jake had told him on the first day of the search there was a possibility they may find him dead from the impact. With that thought in his mind, tears stung his eyes, and he continued his descent to the next bracket.

As he arrived at the next landing he realized that it was a lot smaller than he thought, not to mention that it was at a downward angle which made it extremely difficult to stand while he tried to put in another anchor in the rock wall. As he grabbed the rope to put it in the anchor, the ground gave way. At first he was sliding on small rocks and gravel only inches until there was no ledge and he was falling straight down the side of the cliff. He guessed he had fallen over a hundred feet when he began tumbling through the branches of a tall pine tree. Hitting those branches was a small blessing because it slowed down his momentum enough for him to grab a branch of the tree causing him to land with a hard thud, knocking him unconscious and falling to the ground.

His body hurt from one end to the other as he became conscious. In fact, the more pain he felt, the more conscious he became. "Wow, I survived that fall?" He said considering himself lucky to be alive. As he began to move he felt a sharp pain in his left arm. No doubt that was broken from the fall or the sudden stop at the base of the tree, he wasn't sure which. His pants were torn, with cuts and bruises on this legs. He tried to stand but nearly passed out from the intense stabbing pain he felt in his left leg. *If the leg was broken he was in terrible trouble. He wouldn't be able to finish his search, but worse yet; he would have to be rescued himself.*

Chris took his pants off and tore stripes of cloth out of the left pant-leg material. He looked around and grabbed a couple of sticks to use as braces and fastened them to his leg. It was as much to prevent more damage as it was to assist him in being mobile again. When he finished with the leg he did the same with his arm, although it was more difficult to perform and took him considerably longer to apply the braces with one hand.

As he surveyed the remainder of his body for damages, cuts and bruises, he noticed something shiny about a hundred yards from his location. "Could it be?" His heart skipped a few beats, as he stared at the object reflecting light. Could it be a part of the aircraft wreckage he was seeing?

With a new sense of urgency, he grabbed his backpack and slipped it over his shoulders, taking extra caution over the left arm of course. While slipping into the pack he felt a stinging and burning sensation as the straps ran across the abrasions on the back of his arms and back. He hobbled in the direction of the shiny light. He came to dry branch lying on the ground, retrieved it and broke off one end to form a crude crutch. With each step his anxiety rose until it felt like his stomach was in his throat, making him gulp air.

As he got close he could make out twisted, mangled metal and he could smell the fuel too. Part of him was wishing it was the aircraft wreckage, the other afraid it may be the crash site. By the time he reached the mutilated mess, tears stung his eyes as he recognized a couple call sign letters from one of the wings. "God I hope Dad's alive. I'd give anything to talk with him again." He said aloud to himself, as much as, anyone that was listening. "Anyone here? Anyone alive," he shouted hoping for a response. The silence was deafening.

Chris found an opening in what he thought was the fuselage, big enough to allow him to crawl through, dragging his backpack and first aid supplies behind him. He called out, "Dad, Dad, are you in here?" He stopped to listen. Nothing, except a faint scratching sound. Like someone scratching metal with his fingernails. "Dad, is that you up there?" Chris was half crying and half screaming as he scrambled towards the front of the aircraft in search of his father.

Finally, he made out a figure in front of him. A silhouette that was not moving as Chris reached out and grabbed his father's hand, feeling for a pulse. He didn't feel it at first, but it was there weak and slow, but there.

Chris surveyed his father, taking in his condition. He was pale from blood loss, because of a compound fracture on his right leg, but he was alive. Critically injured, but alive. That's all Chris cared about.

He spoke to his father as he rendered emergency first aid to the wounds. Chris's heart almost stopped beating when his father whispered, "I knew you'd find me." He said with a faint smile.

"Don't talk. Save your energy Dad. I'm going to get you out of here, but I have to get some help first, Okay?"

"Yeah," Dad's voice was barely audible but it created a burst of energy in Chris that he needed.

"Okay, I'm going to signal the rest of the search team and get some more help, okay? Hang in there and we'll get you out of here very soon, Dad."

Chris turned the radio on, and called into it for his brother. No answer came. Again he repeated the message, and still there was no response. He adjusted the squelch button hoping it would give him the additional range he needed to contact another member of the search party. Nothing.

He grabbed his father's hand and said, "I'll be right back, Okay? I can't reach them from inside the wreckage." He crawled and pushed himself through the mangled aircraft, this time working his way out of the wreckage. When he emerged, he had so much excitement he jumped to the ground, wincing in pain from his own injuries. He grabbed the radio and shouted into it. Static was all he heard.

Finally, a voice sounded on the radio. The squelch was more audible than the person speaking but the voice was Jake. Chris had tears of joy falling down his cheeks as he relayed to his brother that their father was alive and in need of more advanced medical care. Jake said, "I'm glad you were right Chris. I know where you are, we're on our way. Keep him alive until we get there."

Chris's heart skipped a beat as he heard them repeat the message. More tears came rushing out as he realized for the first time that everything was going to be alright. Things were finally turning around and going in the right direction for a change.

Driving Safely in Nevada

By Particia Kranish

"We're going camping," the kids sang a couple of hundred times.

"Maybe you'll meet Yogi Bear." That was Es in her fake husky movie star voice. They cheered the possibility. "You might even run into a grizzly bear."

"I love bears," Nicky said.

"I'm sure they love you too. For lunch."

"A bear would throw up if it ate you."

"Okay, that's it, no more arguing. There are no bears where we're going."

We had immigrated from the gritty Lower East Side of New York to the lush green hills of northern California. It was 1975 and we were now bona fide citizens of the City of Berkeley, eligible to stay at Berkeley's proletariat answer to Lake Tahoe, the pay what you can, Sierra Nevada Family Camp. Fifty dollars for one week was my opening bid. The camp official wrote it in her ledger. *Mother and four children: Es, fourteen. Sam, ten. Nicky, eight. Bird, four. $50.*

"Anyone else in your family?"

"Just us," we said.

She gave us a brochure with a postage sized map and a blurry view of the lake. The camp was "excited to offer the green chair circle, a staff show, quiet hours, table night, tie-dye and theme days." We didn't know what any of that meant, but we knew we wanted to be a part of it. The city even provided free transportation for people who didn't have cars. I said thank you very much, but we can get there on our own. Not that I had a car or a license, but I had $600 and needed a cheap way to get us to Las Vegas. Es quoted from her tattered copy of *Zen and the Art of Motorcycle Maintenance*, "Sometimes it's better to travel than to arrive."

"We'll do both," I said. "We'll drive *and* arrive. No sweat."

"Sure," Es raised one eyebrow. "You're wonder mom."

The next day Sam said, "I got us a map of Desolation Wilderness."

"Why would we want that?"

"Because, *Esther*, that's where we're going!"

Nicky and Bird said, "Yay." Es said, "I think we're already there."

I coerced a friend with an old Mustang to let me practice steering in a straight line. I kept my hands on the wheel, my eyes on the road, and my right foot from stepping on my left. Choke, stick shift, and clutch had such negative vibes. An automatic, I reasoned, would practically drive itself. I took the test, which was to drive around a few deserted blocks in Oakland, pull over, put the car in reverse, remain parallel to the curb for about twenty yards, and park on a steep side street. I lost points for not angling my front wheels against said curb. A miss is as good as a mile my Mustang friend said, happy to rid herself of her overconfident student. License and money in hand, we headed to the used car dealer.

The cheapest car on the lot was a 1965 Ford Falcon. It sported a wide chrome grid and a steering wheel as big as a manhole cover. It was Mustang's bigger brother decked out in sixties splendor. Es would sit in the front with me. Bird would squeeze between the boys in the back. In case of a rear-end collision the three youngest would secure each other like human bubble wrap. The manual was long gone, but Ford, the erstwhile makers of the Pinto, assumed a little danger made you more alert at high speeds. It was time to master crucial navigational skills. Maps covered our kitchen table. My finger traced the route over the squiggly lines that represented the mountains and over the straight line that was the California Nevada border. "Look Es, this is how we'll get there."

"Easy as falling off a cliff," she said.

My kids' father played the Flamingo Lounge, hence our Las Vegas destination. Blue managed to keep a decent roof over his head and some seriously bad food on the table. What the heck, with fifty cent shrimp cocktails available twenty four hours a day (unlimited saltines on the side) no one would actually starve. Whatever the drawbacks, summer was here, school was out and he was home during the day. He promised to keep an eye on them at all times. He didn't say how his other eye was occupied. Roving I guess.

Es had no friends in Berkeley, hated Las Vegas summers, and refused to be babysat while her father was at work. She said her sister and brothers were raised by wolves and sulked on the front porch when they came in from our wildly overgrown Berkeley yard. She couldn't easily escape their company in Las Vegas where an afternoon stroll to the 7-Eleven brought on heat stroke. Her hair was in a great pouf of an Afro, as soft and luminous as a dandelion sphere, and for reasons we didn't dare ask, she had taken to dressing like an underfed lumberjack. Whether it rained or the brilliant California sun flooded the landscape she wore overalls and a red plaid version of a hair shirt.

Two days before lift-off, and we were almost ready.

"Es, please help Bird pack." I divided our camp clothes into five separate piles of jeans, shorts, t-shirts, sweatshirts, and sneakers. The boys wore the same size but Nicky's had worn knees, and mud stains worthy of a Tide commercial. Es walked by where the clothes waited, went into the room she shared with Bird and closed the door.

"I can do it myself," Bird said and pulled a pair of just ironed shorts from the bottom of her pile. The whole stack fell on the floor. "Uh, oh," she said. "I think I need help."

When Bird started walking at a bandy-legged eight months she looked like a roadrunner ready for take off. By four she had developed complex language skills and a voice that carried like a midget opera singer, the perfect foil for two teasing brothers and an impatient older sister.

"Okay darling, let's get your backpack."

I opened the girls' door. Es was on her bed.

"What's that your reading, Es?" She waved the book in the air.

Bird put two shirts in her backpack, and took her favorite sequined tutu from the closet. "That won't fit in your bag honey," I said.

She put a plastic rhinestone tiara on her head, "Can I take this?"

"Do you even know what camp is?" Es pronounced *camp* like we were headed for the *Gulag Archipelago*.

Bird took her new underwear with the iron-on name tags from her dresser drawer. She sighed with exaggerated weariness. "Can I go back outside now?" I nodded yes and she was gone.

Es had my old green and yellow paperback, dragged all the way across country with about a thousand other books I couldn't part with. "Wow, Native Son. That's heavy."

"He ain't heavy. He's my brother." She didn't lift her eyes from the page.

"Right," I said and pulled Es's backpack from the closet and took it into the kitchen to finish packing. *Desolation*

Wilderness, here we come.

At 6:00 a.m. on Saturday morning we checked to make sure we didn't forget anything.

"All systems go," Nicky said.

The Falcon carried us through the High Sierras like we were baby birds safe in its mobile nest. It was still morning when we got to the camp. The preternaturally cheery staff welcomed us and gave us a hand drawn looking map with an X on the spot for our tent, and dotted lines to the facilities. We breathed in the mountain air. Amazing. Thrilling. Euphoric. "Altitude sickness," said Es.

We stowed our things and the boys took off to explore. "Stay together," I said through our tent flap.

Es claimed her cot and pulled her latest existential novel of angst out of her bag. Bird tugged on my arm to come on and join the fun.

" We'll have a wonderful time here, Es. There are so many things to see and learn." Bird was now hanging on my arm with both feet off the tent floor.

"Just like home," Es said.

The camp was everything the brochure said it was. Bird wore her tiara atop her wayward curls and a necklace of macaroni beads. The boys got to hang with the big guys, the teen camp counselors who radiated healthful goodness and patience. At night we sat around the fire singing *If You're Happy and You know It*, roasting marshmallows and trying not to swallow the swarming insects. Later, snug in our sleeping bags, by the light of a Coleman lantern, we read to each other out loud: *Call of the Wild, A Thousand Mile Walk, You Can't Get There From Here.* Four out of five people in our tent were happy. Es, the fugitive from unfresh air, and wildlife that came in every color as long as it was gray, was the lone holdout.

When our week was up, Sam and Nicky hugged their new friends good-bye, threw their crusty camp shorts in an army surplus duffle bag, took the window seats and whispered something I couldn't hear. Bird howled, "No monkey in the middle!"

"Please don't tease your sister."

They snickered like cartoon villains.

"Off to Las Vegas," I said.

The back seat cheering squad erupted. Es rolled her eyes, pained to her soul by the cacophony in the rear. They were her father's eyes translated to her narrow face, beautiful, moist, amber brown, and sad-sweet. All the kids had them, except for the sad part. The boys hid tire-flattened frogs in their pockets and told excruciating stories in funny voices. Bird danced on the kitchen table and smiled brilliantly and cried heartbreakingly. In a family of spotlight grabbing performers, Es was behind the scenes: the script girl, the ripped wardrobe mender, hidden in the dark and focusing the light on the stars of the show.

I reached over to touch her. "You'll see your friends in New York as soon as we can afford it." She made a little *swwt* sound, pulling as far away from me as she could in the wide bench seat of the Falcon. "And that will be?" She paused. "Never," she answered.

She was right. We barely covered our rent. We got a lot of our food from a place that sold dented cans and wilted vegetables in bulk. B.C., before the car, we carried bags up the hills, used an old stroller as a shopping cart and juggled what we could in our arms. Even Bird, ousted from her ride, insisted on carrying stuff. *Anybody seen the plums? Where do you* think *you put the potatoes down? Nicky, if you didn't eat the grapes where are they?*

Now as members of the traveling class our horizons were expanding.

"Everybody in?" I pressed down on the door locks.

"Yep." "Yep." "Yeth." "Obviously."

We pushed out of the gravel drive of the campground and headed for the highway. We had three sleeping bags—the kids had to share—a red gas can in the trunk, a water jug on the roof, backpacks, pillows, blankets, Oatios, peanut butter, crackers, apple slices, and a wide thermos of drinking water, its screw on cup missing. Sam my oldest boy had been a cub scout back home. He was in charge of the compass. The mountains surrounding South Lake Tahoe hemmed the camp. We climbed from 7,000 feet to 11,000 feet. According to Sam's topographical calculations, the terrain was all downhill after that.

A left turn, a right turn, a left turn, another right turn, a few sightseeing stops along the way, soon we are sailing up

US 395. Good-bye High Sierras. Hello open road. We had traveled two hundred miles. Okay, it had taken ten hours, but the educational benefit of woodsy rest stops and extreme ant close-ups was invaluable. We turned east on Nevada 266. We'd stop for the night in Hawthorne, then take the scenic route to Las Vegas: the atomic test range to the east, Death Valley to the west. A battered marker in the shape of a shield mysteriously read NF 026.

The car felt heavier than when we left. The springs groaned. *Sorry buddy*, I sent it a silent message, *we'll lighten up on the way back.* The Falcon, with its massive eight-cylinder engine and steam shovel build had the temperament of an overloaded mule, loyal yes, but ultimately bound by its baser nature. Balking was only a warning. Ignore it and get kicked in the face.

The dappled green of tall pines faded to sage and brown. Cattle crossing signs alerted drivers to straying cows. The Falcon hiccupped. It gasped for breath. The sun dipped behind a hill, winked, then disappeared. We were alone on a two lane road. We could see only as far as the narrow beams of our headlights. Smoke leaked from the seams around the hood. A smell of burning rust seeped through the air vents. If we were a fighter plane, we would be losing altitude about now. The exhausted Falcon stumbled onto the rough shoulder of the road and expired.

Cattle! Our city ears could hear them lowing in the darkness. My ex-cub scout, animal lover and guardian of the flashlight jumped out of the back seat. Sam was small for his age, no bigger than his eight-year-old brother, yet he managed to be officious and reckless at the same time.

"What's that noise?" He waved the light into the infinite desert as he ran past the passenger side. "I hear cows," he said as if that was a good thing, then aimed his light on the front of the car. "Pop the hood."

"Get back inside." He ignored me and pointed to the latch. The car was as hot as a pizza oven. I got out, "Sam! Don't touch anything."

He rushed to the driver's side, reached past me and pulled the release. The bull trapped under the hood bellowed louder. *Aha*, I thought. We weren't the target of an enraged bovine after all, only stuck who knows where in a car that was about to explode. In our pamphlet, *Driving Safely in Nevada,* we learned that without water, mummification initiates in seven hours. Or you completely mummify in seven hours. I couldn't remember which. We, however, had not neglected to fill our regulation five-gallon white plastic container. I fumbled around on the roof rack. It was there. I just couldn't see it. Hadn't I secured the bungee cord when we stopped for gas and a side trip to the Miner's Shoe Museum in Bridgeport? I checked our liquid inventory: two half pints of milk, a quart of orange juice, and drinking water nestled in melting ice. Our blood still pumped through us. Spit still lubricated our throats. (I could tell by the kids' phlegmy breathing.) Except for Sam, they had all fallen asleep on the slow ride. The boiled over engine roar was subsiding, though the hot metal pinged and groaned. I asked Sam to shine his trusty light on the roof. He held it with two hands and panned slowly across. "What are we looking for Mom?"

"Just checking, honey." I didn't want to worry him; after all he was the most avid reader of *How Not to Die in the Desert* material. I expected that our lifeline would miraculously be there, that I had somehow overlooked it. Sam dropped the flashlight but instead of going dark, his face was illuminated. His eyes and mouth were little o's of surprise. A single headlight was aimed at us. Dogs barked hysterically. I could see them now, their ears and hunting dog mouths flapping as they ran towards us. A man moving in warped dreamscape speed held the kind of light they use in movies to blind some hapless schnook just before they shoot him. In his other hand, unreasonably large, and pointing right at us, was a long barreled gun.

"Get in the car Sam!" He froze like a jackrabbit caught in high beams. I wanted to grab him, throw him in the car, and get us all out of there. I didn't move. The man came right up to us, and the beagle-looking dogs stopped barking, better to hear the command to attack. We were definitely off the reservation and Custer was getting his revenge at last.

Just off the road small windows lit up one by one. A house hung in the darkness like a mirage. He holstered his six-shooter. "Hi there," he said.

Sam's face rearranged itself. "Hi," he answered.

"What happened here?"

"Our car was smoking and then it died." Sam's eyes swept over the big man dressed in boots, jeans, and a Stetson—and that gun so dangerously attractive to a ten year old. He had stepped into a cowboy movie and he knew his part.

Sam picked up his junior flashlight, turned it off and stood next to the man who raised our hood and looked at the jumble of hoses and cables and whatever it was that made the car go when you pressed on the gas. We were heading towards Las Vegas I told him. "That's three hundred miles from here," he said. Nothing in his voice suggested that I was a complete idiot, or why we were in a place that was only useful to test atom bombs or to spy UFOs. All the kids' eyes were open now. Es looked as neutral as a mannequin. Nicky and Bird had the dreamy just woke up from a nap in a strange bed look. No one asked where they were or why a house on wheels had mysteriously appeared in the desert night. They got out of the car, and stood alongside the dogs as politely attentive as when the camp director showed them how to make a lariat out of plastic strips and a wooden spool. The man, Mr. Smith I'll call him, took a rag out of his pocket, a cowboy's big bandana in my memory. Maybe he was a cowboy but he wasn't alone. A woman appeared in the miniature doorway of the trailer. "That's my wife," he said. "Why don't you and the kids go inside?"

Before I could react, they took off, Es in the back, Bird and Nicky in the middle, Sam, as usual, in the lead. I couldn't see their faces and they avoided mine—their strategy for doing something before I could say no. We entered the small house—a toy cast adrift in an alien sandbox. Outside were guns, dogs, darkness, and grit, a part of the Nevada landscape that I'd never seen in the Las Vegas of Terrible Herbst and flags the size of circus tents. Beyond the straight and familiar roads between cities was the rest of the universe, bigger, like the kids said, than infinity times infinity.

Close up, the woman was young, pretty in a Ladies Home Journal way. Two aluminum hairclips anchored her bangs. She wore slippers and a flowered housecoat. It was after midnight. I patted my own hair and would have whipped out a brush if I had one handy to smooth the kids' unruly curls. The wood-grained Formica built-ins gleamed. Bird sat down as if this was her first formal dinner and any slip in behavior would get her tossed out. She crossed one dimpled knee over the other. I hoped that she wouldn't wet her pants on the candy colored cushions.

"Would you like some soda?" I mentally telegraphed them, *Say no thank you*. "Yes," they all said together.

Mrs. Smith gave each of them a paper cup and offered me tea.

I said yes too.

Mr. Smith came back in with two other men and what looked like my engine. They put it in the sink. "Can't cool it down too fast or the block will crack." Mr. Smith's friends never looked up, they just went back outside to work on the Falcon.

"Are these all your kids?"

"All mine."

"We have two kids staying at my mother's in Thorne. I came here to keep my husband company."

"Does he work out here?" I tried not to sound too nosy, too New York aggressive. Or California open to anything friendly. Mr. Smith came back, took off his hat and sat down.

"Oh no, we don't live in our RV," she laughed. "We came here because there was some trouble."

"Trouble?"

"Some black guys from the base were coming around. We thought we could help."

"That's how we do things here," Mr. Smith smiled. "We help people."

My big black engine part sat in their sink, and their invitation to use the bathroom (my innards were seized up at that point) was downright hospitable. *Please enjoy your beverage before we kill you and bury you in the sand.* My brown kids made themselves at home. They were all caught in the grand adventure of drinking Dr. Pepper in the middle of the night. Up close, Mr. Smith looked like Jimmy Dean. Not the dead actor, but the sausage guy. What did we look like to them? A hippy family from the East by way of Berkeley, wearing our splattered tie-dyed shirts, stranded on an old road that ran between a desolate expanse of ammo dumps, randomly dotted with gun-toting vigilantes who lay in wait to ambush black soldiers who unwisely wandered off base. To do what? Steal their gold and their womenfolk? Rustle cattle? Poison the well?

Mr. Smith helped his friends grapple the engine block out the tiny door. In an hour the car was humming again. "You're at Lucky Boy Pass now. Look here," he pointed down the hill, "those lights down there are Hawthorne. The road twists and turns, so take it slow, and you'll get there in an hour. There's an auto repair shop not far from the motel. Opens in the morning. Ask for Jack. Tell him we think the thermostat needs replacing. Probably the radiator too. Okay?"

"Yes," I said. "Thank you so much."

We got in the car and it started right up. Sam, Bird, and Nicky waved at Mrs. Smith and her husband until, one by one, the windows in the trailer blinked out. The stars and the distant lights of Hawthorne lit the way.

We got to the motel at 3 a.m. I carried Bird. The rest of the kids staggered to the front desk. I was so grateful to see the pasty-faced clerk I wanted to cover his face with kisses.

"Mom," Sam said.

"Mom," he said again. I looked at him. *What now?*

"It smells like gym socks in here."

Well, let's go to the Ritz instead.

"Don't worry about it, Sam."

"Mom," Es pulled on my arm as I was trying to sign my credit card receipt. "Nicky's got his face on the floor." Nicky was lying flat out on the maroon carpet. Even in the dim fluorescent light I could see it was filthy. I tried to balance Bird on my hip by leaning on the counter but her head kept slipping off my shoulder. She was sliding towards the carpet too. Sam kept watch through his drooping lids. My steadfast tin soldier.

Es kept her hand on my arm. It took all my energy to work up a smile. "This is a Worst Western Hotel." The look on her face said we had driven straight to hell.

The desk clerk gave me the key and pointed past the green neon sign that had beckoned us a few minutes earlier. "They have a vacancy," Es said. "What a surprise."

We stumbled out of the lobby, our feet crunching on a moving carpet of beetles. Nicky held onto my skirt. He was asleep, but at least he was upright. I left the Falcon parked where it was, loaded with our stuff. The small black predators escorted us to our room. There were two beds, a sink in the corner, and a bathroom with a door that didn't quite shut. We peeled off our clothes and got into the beds in our underwear, the girls with me, the boys in the other. Pillows under our heads, an air conditioner rattling in the window, for now, we slept in the Ritz of the desert.

The sun was blazing when we got to the garage. In the one mile drive from the motel our just-showered optimism melted. Our Falcon was already overheating.

Jack shook his head. "It'll take a couple of days to get the parts in." Today was Sunday. I was very, very lucky he said that he was there, but he couldn't do anything without the parts.

"I have to get to Las Vegas today."

He shook his head. "There's a bus leaving at midnight. It'll get you there in the morning. Honestly ma'am this car's not going anywhere right now."

"Leave the Falcon?"

"Leave the Falcon," he said. "Take the Greyhound."

We spent the desultory day exploring Hawthorne, then trudging back to the motel coffee shop. "Another soda? Sure, why not?" The casino was off limits to children. Even the hardware store's Shovel Exhibit was closed on Sundays. Nicky seemed crushed that he would miss his two favorite things: dirt and tools used to dig in the dirt.

We studied the beetles instead. New York roaches took a siesta. Their ubiquitous Nevada cousins were active day and night. Was there a Queen Beetle? Were there worker beetles, and if so, were they unionized? Tough little guys, when you squashed one (only by accident the boys swore) it oozed a white paste, then reanimated itself, and toddled off like Fearless Fosdick. *A mere flesh wound.*

At midnight we boarded the Greyhound bus. I held Bird in my lap. I could feel her heart beating through her damp cotton undershirt. She was limp with exhaustion. We all were. After a bleak pit stop on I-95 I fell asleep too. Not even the allure of a Dr. Pepper in the middle of the night roused us.

Sometime before morning I heard music, a lullaby

played on a wind chime. I jerked awake when I realized that Bird wasn't in my lap. Sam was asleep next to me, the worried look still on his face. I searched up and down the aisle. Nicky slumped in the seat in back of mine, his head bouncing gently on the armrest. Through the narrow slit between the seats Es's skin was rosy in the predawn desert light. She cradled her sister in her arms and was singing to her. Bird was awake, as intent on her sister's face as a lip reader. Es's voice (when had it grown up?) was a supple whisper, sweetening the dreams of the sleeping passengers. The rocking bus hummed an accompaniment and the tires spun in time with the melody.

> *When I miss your smiling face*
> *I simply close my eyes,*
> *And I'm held in your embrace,*
> *And dream I'm by your side.*
> *No matter how far I roam,*
> *I promise to be true.*
> *Where you are is my home,*
> *I will return to you.*

At the Rainbow's End

By Jeffrey Segal and T.C. Contin

The grey sky pissed out a steady stream of rain dissolving the horse shit into brown puddles. Colin gripped his frayed jacket together and trudged down Boston's filthy streets. His feet knew the way to both warmth and comfort.

"There you be, Colin. Thought the blasted rain got the better of you." Sliding a shot to his favorite customer, the barkeep was always quick with a drink and a smile.

Colin lifted the dirty glass to his mouth and jerked his wrist back. The whisky warmed his cold body. "Another, Joseph. If you please." His squinting eyes adjusted to the dim light of the bar. Cheerful song filled the space masking the despair of its singers. Drink would do the same for Colin.

Cheap perfume drifted through the air. "I can help you forget your troubles, Colin." Warm hands caressed his sore muscles helping to turn back the hours of working on the dock.

He turned and smiled, "That you could. But not my

wife and baby. Thanks, love, for the offer."

She leaned over, her breasts almost spilling out, and kissed him. "That Sarah is a lucky one."

He watched her as she made her way back through the crowd; every man's eyes followed the same path. If song and drink didn't relieve their misery, sex would.

He downed the second shot just as quickly and ordered another hoping it would ease his mind. The small bar filled with workers bringing in the smell of the sea and the sweat of their labor.

He gripped the wet glass, but it slipped and landed on the lap next to him.

"You blasted Mick!" The large man stood and shoved Colin out of his seat.

"I have to take that from the Italians and Brits, but not me own, Sean." Colin's fist slammed the man's jaw.

Sean spit a bloody tooth on the floor. "You'll pay for that," and punched him in the gut.

A spew of whiskey and vomit erupted. Colin wiped his mouth and staggered back. His shaky hands grabbed a broken chair leg. He clubbed the man. Blood stained the wood and splattered everywhere.

Joseph pulled out a shotgun. "Tis enough! This is me pub not the ring."

Colin grabbed a paper from the bar and wiped the blood off; red smeared across the hopeful announcement of striking it rich out West. "How 'bout a pint this time, Joseph?"

The dark beer sat untouched as he read the flyer again. "What kind of fools do they take us for?"

Joseph answered, "Me brother just sent word he did indeed find gold. Plans to come back a rich man."

Colin's eyes grew wide with the thought. "You don't say."

"Aye, that I do. I know of many lads who've gone out West."

The rest of his night was filled with hopeful thoughts and alcohol.

His feet were clumsy but his heart light as he tripped up the flight of battered wooden stairs. Heart pounding from the effort and excitement of gold, he reached the top landing and patted down his pockets. "Forgot the blasted key," and he rapped happily on the door.

It opened before he had the chance to knock again. "Are you daft? It's after twelve. You'll wake the baby."

As if on cue, a wail filled the small space. Emptiness filled both the entry way and Colin's hopes.

When Sarah returned, she held a small bundle wrapped in a pink blanket. She swayed back and forth and whispered angrily, "Why in heavens are you so late?"

"I have something to tell you, Sarah."

"And don't tell me you weren't at the pub 'cause I smell it on you."

His face flushed with anger trying to remember the

news and the feeling, but both faded away like gold at the end of a rainbow. "'Tis nothing now. You ruined it." He plodded across the floor and collapsed on the bed.

Sarah sighed and placed the baby down. She knelt and removed her husband's shoes and socks. Her hands caressed his muscular body and lightly brushed the dark hair from his face. "Why can't we be enough for you?" She kissed him lightly before leaving the room.

The incessant squawking of the gulls bore into his brain. He dragged himself out of bed and stumbled into the other room.

"'Bout time," Sarah said while nursing the baby. "There's some porridge and soda bread on the table."

"Thanks." Filling a glass of brown-tinged water, he sat down with a thump and gobbled the food.

"Sarah, I tried to tell you something last night, but you wouldn't listen."

Her brows rose over skeptical blue eyes.

"I'm damn tired of a lousy job on the docks and living in this dump. Tired of seeing 'No Irish Need Apply' signs to every decent job."

Sarah placed the baby in her basket. "We're all right, and saving enough to move someday. Some lads don't even have jobs."

"Not good enough. I can make some real money out West."

Sarah faced him hands on her hips. "You'd leave us?" Her voice rose. "For what?"

"For gold, Sarah. For a chance."

"Gold? And what do you know about finding gold?"

"Nothing. Yet. But, I know I can do this."

"No, Colin, don't go. Think about it a few days. Please."

He looked down and nodded.

"I'm taking the baby out for some fresh air."

"No fresh air around here," he said.

When Colin heard the click clack of feet going down the stairs, he went to the closet and filled a burlap sack with clothes. He felt around for the small metal box kept behind a board in the closet and left half the cash. "Mary, Mother of God, please forgive me." He found an old pencil and yellowed piece of paper.

Dearest Sarah.

Please understand. I'm doing this for us. There's money enough. Go live with your sister 'cross town. She married up. I'll write soon. I love you!

Yours forever,

Colin.

He crept down the stairs, eyes searching and looking back at their flat. "I'll miss you, Sarah. But not this."

Colin walked the damp streets to the train yard. Men worked the tracks, bodies glistening with the sweat of labor, while bums still slept under newspaper covers. He bought his ticket and waited with other restless passengers until the iron horse rumbled in.

He gazed at the track leading to new places; the thrill of adventure quickened his heart. The massive train was too small to contain his hope. He paced up and down the aisles looking at mothers rocking their sleeping babies to the steady rhythm of the train.

Stretching out his weary body, Colin rubbed the dew covered window and saw a rainbow arching across the land. "I know I can do this." The train sped ever closer to the rainbow's end.

The countryside changed with each passing day, as lush fields of green faded to grey barren lands on his journey westward. The mountains, huge jagged rocks of red and brown, swallowed the empty valleys. He slept now dreaming of gold.

***

Colin trudged from the small Nevada town leading his mule sagging with equipment and headed toward streams where other prospectors panned for gold. Shading his eyes from the brilliance of the sun, he glanced at the men digging for gold in the hills above. Sweat dripped down his face and his clothes stuck to him. Things did not look promising. Suspicious stares followed him as he moved away from the others and settled near a few scraggly trees.

"Not much shade out here. Where ya from?"

Colin turned, facing a large man with long, shaggy hair

that matched his beard.

"What's it to you?"

"Whoa there, partner. People don't take kindly to strangers 'round these parts, 'til they get to know 'em."

"Aye," Colin said.

"Irish are ya?"

Colin's jaw tightened. The man stepped back. "Somethin' wrong with that?"

"Not unless you make it so. I'm Sam."

"Colin."

Sam strolled over to the mule. "Ya spent yerself a right pretty penny. Any experience prospecting?"

"Not really."

"Good luck. You'll need it."

***

Colin felt his beard and ran his red, calloused fingers through his long hair. Been here three months and Sarah wouldn't recognize him. He sat on a wooden crate, hands shaking, and read her letter again.

Dearest Colin,

We moved in with Catherine, and I miss you even more. You shouldn't have snuck out like you did. A proper goodbye it should've been. Ben offered you a good job. Don't be letting your pride get in the way. You're needed here. You missed Shannon's first birthday. Stop searching for gold. Come back to us. Please.

All my love,

Sarah

He put down the letter. His head sunk into both hands.

***

Another two months produced nothing of value, and he moved his search farther away from the others. He didn't pan anymore, and his back and arms ached from the pounding of the pick. Then while searching what looked like an old riverbed above a ravine, he uncovered a large, heavy nugget. "Thank you Jesus, Mary, and Joseph!" He stuffed it into his sack.

He rushed to town and found the assayer's office. A thin man sat hunched over a neatly organized desk with a nameplate that read, "Cecil Higginbottom."

Colin yanked out the rock and asked, "What's this worth?"

Boney fingers fondled the nugget. "Come back in a few hours."

Colin filled two anxious hours with thoughts of wealth. After checking the clock in the general store for the twelfth time, he tried to slow his pace as he entered the office.

"This must be your lucky day. Has about twenty ounces of high grade gold. I can give you $180 cash."

"Twenty ounces," Colin said. "$250 is what it's worth."

"If you want me to pay you now, it's $180. Or get a bank note."

"I'll take the blasted cash now." Walking away he mumbled, "You're an ass."

Heading back to the same place, he faced the hill of rock where the nugget was found. He lifted his pick with renewed vigor; the rhythmic sound echoed through the hills. Trading the pick for his sledgehammer, the pounding continued until replaced by the roar of falling rocks. When the dust cleared, Colin stared into a hole that revealed a cavern. "Maybe this *is* my lucky day."

There was enough light to see inside, and Colin carefully squeezed through. With several swings of the pick, some rocks fell away from the inside wall. He put a few in his sack and used the others to hide the opening.

Gold was there for the taking.

Colin raced back to the assayer's office.

Cecil squinted from the burst of sunlight flooding the dark office. "Where'd you find these rocks so fast?"

"How much?"

"They're the same quality as before. Same rate, but get a bank note from now on."

"Aye." He smiled and left to find better company.

Colin frequented the saloon before, but not to celebrate. He was on his third shot when Sam sat down next to him.

"Barkeep. Give my friend here a drink."

"Found something, partner?"

"A few rocks worth something. That's all."

"Be careful 'bout who you trust. Here comes Mollie trying to get some of yer money."

"Howdy, Sam. Nice to see your new friend again." She winked at Colin. "Is there anything I can do for you?" She laughed. "Or to you?"

Excitement grew in his pants. "A drink for my new friend here Mollie. A pint for me and get Sam whatever he wants."

A couple hours later Colin returned home drunk and satisfied.

The next day, he headed out carrying two picks and his bag slung over his shoulder.

Sam came up to him chuckling. "Getting a late start today, Colin? Seems like yer doin' okay now. Take care. If ya ever need some advice, let me know."

"I'll keep that in mind."

All through the week Colin's luck continued, and he wondered how to keep all his gold safe.

***

"Mornin', Sam. I may need a wee bit of help."

With a cocky smile, he patted Colin on the back. "How can I help ya?"

"Money," Colin said. "Equipment, the claim, and even Chinamen workers. 'Tis all too much."

"Try the bank?"

Colin shrugged. "They'd loan me some, but I'd be workin' for them."

"Tell ya what. We'll be partners. It worked for me before. I'll help you work it and give you my *expertise.*" Sam grinned. "We'll split the profits fifty-fifty."

"I'm not a bloody fool. That's not much better than the bank."

"It's better. Ya get my help. And my money. Don't ya trust me?"

"Eighty-twenty split," Colin said. "Take it or leave it."

"Okay. Whatever you say partner."

Greed began to swirl through his soul like gold in river pans, replacing his dreams of Sarah, and his lust for it fueled his every thought. He was up again before the sun and wasted no time heading out to the mine leaving Sarah's unopened letter still lying on the dresser.

"Hey there, partner!" A voice cut through the morning's silence.

"Jesus Mary Mother of God! Don't you be creeping up on me, Sam."

Laughter echoed off the hills. "Another early start? The Chinamen ain't even up yet."

"Aye . Working the vein you found the other day."

Sam slapped the dirt off his pants. "That's a right good idea. Just don't go digging your own grave."

The lonely cave welcomed Colin. He rubbed his raw hands over the cool rock. "Be good to me today," he whispered sweetly.

Sam pointed down the short tunnel. "Try over there."

"Is it safe?"

"Trust me, today's a lucky day." He strolled to the entrance. "I'm takin' a break."

The morning sky turned light blue as Sam left the mine.

He paused as the roaring sound erupted through the dark mouth of the collapsing cave. It coughed out bits of rock and dust.

Sam whistled as he walked away.

Gold *was* there for the taking.

Happy Endings

By Steve Fey

Why hasn't he called me? It's after noon and he said he'd be done by eleven-thirty at the latest." Taylor stared at the screen of her phone as she strode across campus. She stopped in her tracks when Justin's face appeared.

"Hello?"

"Taylor, I'm so sorry! Old Adams called an emergency TA meeting about some cheating sophomores and he wouldn't even let me call you to explain."

"Oh, I'm sorry, Justin!" Taylor gushed.

"Huh? You didn't do anything wrong. Did you?"

"Oh. No. I was thinking about something when you called. You still want to grab lunch at the Union?"

"Sure, but is it okay if Marty comes along?"

"Why wouldn't that be okay?" she asked.

"I wanted to make sure," Justin said. "We can be there in five minutes."

"See you!" Taylor pushed disconnect and shoved the phone into her pocket. She sat on an empty concrete bench.

"Hey, Taylor," Marty shouted as he and Justin walked up a few minutes later. "How's it going?"

Justin leaned down and kissed her on her left cheek. "Hi, sweets," he said.

"About time you got here," she smiled at Justin.

"I told him you'd be pissed," Marty said. "You hate being late almost as much as I do."

"You looked pretty serious when we walked up," Justin said. "What's up?"

"That internship at UMC," she said. "There's a lot to do if I want to have a chance of getting it."

"Justin was telling me about how he's trying to get his book published," Marty said.

Taylor laughed, "Oh, yes, the Glacknow book. It's been a decade in the making, and it's still not published."

"Don't remind me!" Justin said. "The thing is, it's good now. Not like that drivel I made you guys read back in grade school."

"That Writers' Workshop you took help you any?" Marty asked.

"Like I said, don't ask. It almost made me go back to marketing."

"Shall we go get some lunch?" Taylor asked. They went.

As they were on line to order, Taylor said, "So, I'm

going to be a clinical psychologist, and Justin is going to write the great American novel and be famous. What are you going to do for the rest of your life, Marty?"

Marty laughed. "Have you used the new "What's Happening On Campus?" app on your phone?

"It's the best app ever! Why?"

"Because I wrote it," Marty said, completely deadpan.

"Dude!" Justin said.

"You did not!" Taylor said.

"Did so! It started as an assignment for Software Design 204, but it sort of got out of hand."

"You're getting an 'A', right?" Justin asked.

"I'd better get an 'A'!"

"How about royalties?" Taylor asked.

"For a project that the University took over? Dream on. But, I'm going to leverage that success into a nice, fat career running my own software development company. Here's a table."

"Cool stuff," Justin said. "You got a name for your enterprise?"

"Not yet," Marty said.

Taylor patted Marty's arm. "Nice job," she said. "Wow, you must work out."

Marty grinned. "Only on days that end in 'y'," and winked. Taylor shivered.

"Do you have any idea how badly the average freshman writes?" Justin asked after they were seated.

"It makes sense," Taylor said. "You remember Mister Hudson's English class, right?"

"Oh, yes!" Justin said. "And now I have a hundred and fifty of that sort of paper to read."

"I'd help, but," Marty started to say.

Justin finished his sentence for him. "But you're a geek coder who doesn't know how to spell too!"

"T o!" Marty said.

"T w o," Taylor put in.

"You guys are two too much!" Justin said with a grin.

"I think that was a joke," Taylor said. Marty grinned as Justin shook his head.

"You okay, sweetie?" Justin asked Taylor. "You look like you're cold or something."

Taylor shook her head. "Oh. No. I was thinking about the grant committee."

"So, both of you, take a break," said Marty.

Justin's phone chirped. He looked at the screen. "I wonder who this is." He touched the screen. "Hello?"

Marty and Taylor looked at each other. "You don't suppose?" Marty said.

"That it's good news? Well, look at him!"

Justin's eyes widened as he spoke excitedly. "Really? Sure!"

"Maybe he's finally about to get some good news about that book," Marty said.

"That's wonderful! I'm very happy for him!" Taylor said.

As they watched Justin, Marty and Taylor skootched their chairs closer together. Marty's arm brushed against Taylor's and he quickly skootched his chair away. Justin touched the screen on his phone and looked up.

"You look happy!" Taylor said. "Is the book sold?"

"No," Justin admitted. "But I did get a spot at the Midwestern Writers' Conference."

"A conference of writers? There are more crazy guys like you out there?" Marty asked.

"You're a funny man, dude. I missed the deadline for registration while I was down with Mono last month, so I had to get on a waitlist. That call was from the conference registrar. I'm in!"

"Will you get to pitch those agents and editors you wanted to meet?"

"Absolutely! And sit with them at dinner."

"And that's how you sell a book?"

"Well, that's part of how you sell a book," Justin explained. "Maybe the most important part."

"Dude, we have to celebrate!" Marty said. "Let's ditch this pop stand and go downtown!"

"Is that a good idea during finals week?" Taylor asked.

"It might be for him," Justin said. "He's already a famous software developer. I've got to grade."

"And I have to grade my students' final reports as well," Taylor said, "not to mention that I have a final exam of my own tomorrow."

"I thought you were done with classes," Marty said.

"You remember. I told you that I missed that 500 level lecture on deviant behavior and I'm making it up this term."

"Oh, yeah *deviant* behavior. I remember," Marty said.

"You're such a pervert!" Taylor laughed.

"But loveable," Marty said.

"I have to go to Chicago," Justin said. "So I need to finish my grading today."

"Chicago?"

"It's where the conference is. And it opens Friday morning."

"As in the day after tomorrow?" Taylor asked.

"Yes. And I want to be there for the whole thing. I have to get to McCarran by noon tomorrow to make it to the hotel in time to get some sleep before Friday."

"Not driving?"

"I wish. Two days on the road each way?"

"But you'd get to cross Nebraska," Marty said with a grin.

"I don't think I could meet a potential publisher for my book if I wasn't able to do some research on them first," Taylor said.

"I guess that's why we're together," Justin said as he unwrapped his burger. "Compatible differences."

"Apparently that is so," Taylor said.

"Besides, I've been doing that," Justin added.

"So, you're completely done with marketing then?"

Marty asked. Taylor looked at Marty, then at Justin.

"I guess I am. If I can make a go at writing fiction," Justin's let the thought hang.

"You won't have to write lies about laundry detergent," Marty finished for him.

Justin grinned. "Yeah. Just lies about monsters and monster killers." He bit down on his sandwich.

"You getting enough air with that burger?" Taylor asked. Justin stopped for a second and mumbled, "In a hurry. Gotta rush." What his friends heard was "Immmuh huhhhie gaggaaa rffff." He washed the sandwich down and said, "I have to get to those papers!" He kissed Taylor on the cheek and ran off shouting, "Later, guys!"

Marty watched Justin disappear behind the Chemistry building. "Wow. I never saw him eat that fast before."

"You have to allow for his excitement," Taylor said.

"The book's not sold yet," Marty pointed out.

"But it will be," Taylor said. "Even in third grade I thought it was a good story."

"What about you?" Marty asked as he ate. "If you get that internship will you be a success too?"

"I'll have to see how that goes," Taylor said.

"You could always go back to your art," Marty said.

"Maybe. If I were any good at it."

"I always liked your stuff. I still have that picture of a cat that you drew for me up on my wall in a frame."

"You do?" Taylor touched her cheek. "Oh, Marty, that's so nice!"

"I like pretty stuff," he said.

*****

Justin packed a suitcase with wheels on it. Marty watched.

"Say, dude, any chance I can get a look at that manuscript again?"

"You read the original, right?"

"Come on, you said it was a whole lot better now. I won't steal it. I can't write my way out of a wet paper bag, anyway. Nobody would believe I did a whole book."

"Okay. I gave a copy to Taylor to read last night. I made her swear that she'd never let anyone else see it until the book is published, but for you, sure. I'll tell her you're the exception."

"Thanks, man! I figured that since we've been through so much together,"

"All three of us!" Justin said.

"Yeah. Plus a few other kids we dragged along. Do you believe some of the stuff we got into?"

"I remember someone who almost got shot by an old fart on Ohio Avenue," Justin said.

"Oh, man. That was a night! Is he out yet?"

"Don't know. If you visit home on break you could stop at the police station and ask them."

"Hah! No thanks!"

"Then you may never know. There. That's it!"

"So you're ready to go?"

"Ready."

"You'll be back next Sunday?"

"Yeah. Late afternoon. I'll tell Taylor about the book when I call her. Also maybe that I'm pissed off about her meeting that guy instead of seeing me off."

"Dude, he's the head of the grants committee."

"Whatever. Tell her I'll call when I get there."

"Will do, bro! We'd better go. You wouldn't want to miss the plane."

That evening Marty stopped by to read Justin's manuscript.

"Marty! Hello, come on in," Taylor said when she saw him. "Would you like a beer?"

"Always like a beer," Marty said, "and a look at Justin's book, if possible."

Taylor smiled. "Yes, he called from his hotel. He told me that you were an exception to his absolute secrecy rule."

"Like anyone would believe I could write it if I did try to sell it." She handed him a bottle covered in condensation. "Now that's what I call a cold beer!"

"This place is a dump, but the fridge works quite well," she said. "One second. I'll get you the book." She disappeared into the bedroom and returned with a stack of printed pages.

"How could he afford all the paper and ink?" Marty asked.

"He's been using the printer in the Lit Department office at two in the morning."

"Kind of like where I get my toilet paper, then."

Taylor laughed. "I won't ask."

"Good."

Marty started reading. Then he stopped and drank some beer. "You know," he said, "I think I'll read this over the weekend. I'm too burned out to focus."

"You can't take it home," Taylor said. "Justin said you have to read it here."

"Oh. Well, if you're going to be around tomorrow I'll drop by sometime and have a go at it then."

"I have things to do in the morning. Come by after lunch."

Marty drained his bottle. "Deal. Around one?"

"That would be good."

"Good. I think I'll slog on home and crash out early tonight."

As Taylor let him out, he turned to say goodbye. She was right in front of him, wearing a smile. He took a deep breath.

"Uh, goodnight then," he said.

"Goodnight, Marty," Taylor replied. She closed the door as he turned to walk home. She looked at the closed door for a while before she turned around.

Marty's last thought as he drifted to sleep that night was, "I can't be stealing my best friend's girl. I can't."

He smiled broadly as he knocked on Taylor's door the next day. Taylor and Justin's door, that is.

Taylor opened the door with a smile of her own. "Hi, Marty! Come on in. Would you like some coffee? I made a pot."

Marty bounced into the room, grinning. "Sure! That sounds great!"

He picked up Justin's manuscript from where he'd put it down twelve hours earlier. When Taylor set his cup down on the brick and board end table next to his chair she brushed against his arm with her own. He shivered.

He found the sticky note placeholder he had left and resumed reading. After a minute he said, "I was too tired last night. I didn't see how damned good this is!"

"Yes. Justin is an excellent writer. I expect that he'll be another Stephen King in a few years."

"I don't know about that. King writes horror. This is definitely Sci-Fi Adventure stuff."

"Heinlein, then. Or Asimov."

"I always loved Asimov," he said and looked into her eyes.

"Wait until you see how he gets his hero out of that prison they're about to throw him into," Taylor said.

"I can't wait!" he said and swallowed. He turned his eyes back to the manuscript.

It was so good that when he finally read "THE END" it was after six. He glanced at his watch and gasped.

He looked around the apartment. "You've cleaned the house!"

"I told you it was an excellent book," Taylor said.

"Yeah. I'd say so," Marty replied. "How did I miss you cleaning?"

"You were engrossed in the fictional world created by the author," Taylor explained. "In fact, you were so engrossed that I was able to vacuum, dust, and do two loads of laundry without you noticing."

"Wow. Well, I'm hungry now that I finished it. Want to grab a pizza?"

"I'd love to," she replied. "You buying?"

Marty laughed. "Sure. After you let me sit and read all day, it's the least I can do."

She opened the door. "Then let's go!" Marty walked in front of her. "But not Pagliai's," she continued, "I hate that thin crust!"

"That's okay. Pisanello's is just over on Maryland."

After Taylor closed the door she tripped on a rough spot on the sidewalk and grabbed Marty's arm for support. He heard blood rush in his ears.

"I wish the landlord would fix that," Taylor said. "I'm okay now." She kept one had looped through Marty's arm. Marty patted her hand in the crook of his elbow.

"You cold?" he asked.

"No. I'm fine," she answered.

That night it took a long time for him to drift off to

sleep. At the same time Taylor was lying in her bed staring at the cracked plaster in the ceiling.

*****

"I'd like to see a query and some pages," the editor told Justin. "If you've been writing since fourth grade you must be passionate about your work."

"Third grade, actually. It was in fourth grade that I started letting my friends read my stories."

"Sci-Fi is a great genre. I hope that we can work together," said the editor, offering her hand.

Marty shook her hand and took his leave. As he turned to search for the exit, he ran into another person doing the same thing.

"Oh! I'm sorry!" the person said.

Marty looked at the woman he had run into. He sucked in a quick breath. She was beautiful!

"I'm sorry!" he said.

"Have you seen where we're supposed to leave the room?" the beautiful woman asked.

Justin looked around again and found the back door. "Hey," he said, "I think I have. That way."

"Then they're not locking us in here forever!" She walked toward the exit. Justin turned and walked next to her.

"Do you write?" he asked.

"Oh, yes. I pitched a book to the Harlequin editor. I'm afraid it isn't very good."

"They didn't want to see it?"

The beautiful woman laughed. "That's just it. They do want to see it, and now I'm afraid they'll hate it."

"I'm Justin," he said. He let his hand dangle.

"Kristie," she said, and held out her hand. He took it in his own and stumbled."

"Oops!" Kristie said. "I did that coming down here."

"I guess maybe it's safer to stand still for introductions," he said.

"There's over half an hour until the next session. How about some coffee?" she suggested.

"Sounds great. I'm beat from traveling yesterday."

"I'm lucky. I live here," she said. "Do you have time to see the sights of Chicago before you fly home?"

"You know, I was so excited at getting to come to the conference at the last minute that I didn't think about what else I might do. But I am on break. Maybe I can take an extra day or two. Is Chicago nice?"

"Chicago is way beyond nice! Maybe I'll show you around a bit. If you'd like me to, that is. Here's the hospitality room."

"It's nice of you to take in a stranger," Justin said.

"I'm not taking you in, I'm showing you the city," she laughed.

"Well, you know, you're being most kind," he said as he filled a cup from the urn. "You want anything in it?"

"Chicago girls are tough. I'll take it straight," she looked into his eyes. He held the cardboard cup until it hurt.

"Ow!" he said as he put the cup down next to the urn.

She picked it up along with a corrugated sleeve which she slipped over the cup. "Get yourself one and let's go sit," she suggested.

Justin told Kristie about his sci-fi action adventure book. Kristie told Justin about her swashbuckler romance novel. After a while Justin checked his watch. "Holy crap! It's four-thirty!"

"What?"

"Yes! We've missed the whole afternoon!"

She glanced at the clock on the wall. "I had two workshops down on my "to attend" list."

"Me too! Boy, time sure flies . . ." he left the old saw unfinished.

"When you're having fun? She said as she looked at him.

"Yeah. When you're having fun," he smiled.

*****

Marty walked along the quiet Sunday streets near the University, lost in thought. He bumped into somebody.

"Marty!" Taylor shouted with surprise.

"Taylor?"

"What are you doing walking around like that?"

"I don't know. Maybe the same thing you're doing walking around like that?"

"I'm not certain what I'm doing," she admitted.

"Me neither," he said. "Sometimes I like to walk and

think."

"You're a kinesthetic," she told him.

"What?"

"You think with your feelings. It's not uncommon. For instance, when you lose something, you need to walk around until you remember where it is."

"Wow. You're right. And usually after a while it comes to me! How do you know that?"

Taylor smiled at him. "I am a psychologist, you know." Marty's heart thumped.

"Taylor, you know I've always liked you."

"And I've always liked you, Marty."

Marty swallowed a large lump. "And I have always enjoyed hanging out with you."

"Yes. I enjoy hanging out with you, too."

Marty cleared his throat. "And the last few days, maybe I've enjoyed hanging out with you even more than usual. You know?"

"I do know, Marty. The feeling is mutual." She took Marty's hands in hers. His heart did a flip.

"But, Taylor, you know we have a bit of a problem, right?"

"Justin."

"Yes! He's my oldest friend, from a long time ago. Like forever. And I don't want to hurt him."

"Unfortunately, he's in Chicago. It's difficult to have a conversation with someone who doesn't even call."

"He hasn't called you?"

"He called from his hotel when he arrived, but that was the last time."

"Have you called him?"

"I've left messages that he hasn't returned."

"Taylor, we . . ." he stopped.

"I know, Marty. I never thought . . . but then we've been hanging out since Justin left for New York and . . ."

"Yeah, and, huh?" Marty said. He looked at Taylor for a few seconds, and then gave her a bear hug. Taylor hesitated long enough to take a breath, and then hugged him back.

When they finally broke off Marty looked in Taylor's eyes and she looked into his.

"Remember that time we broke into that house and collected evidence to get the old guy arrested?" she asked. That's when Marty kissed her.

After the kiss, Taylor said, "That can't happen again."

Marty said, "I know."

"Poor Justin."

"We haven't done anything."

"He's living in my apartment!"

"Maybe he'll move to Chicago permanently."

"It doesn't matter where he lives. He is our oldest friend. We need to consider how our being in a relationship would affect him."

"He wouldn't be happy about it."

Taylor said, "It would perhaps be for the best if we

pretended that we never almost . . ."

"We didn't even 'almost'."

"No. That's true," she took a deep breath, "so if we go back to simply being good friends, nothing needs to change."

"Exactly."

Taylor pulled out her phone. She pushed a button and a few seconds later said, "Justin, this is Taylor. Please call me!"

"Good. That never happened?" Marty asked.

"Never happened," she said.

*****

Justin glanced at his phone and furrowed his forehead.

"What's the matter?" Kristie asked.

"It's Taylor. The friend I share a place with. She's called four times in the last few hours."

"Are you two . . .?"

"We're old friends. We never talked about the arrangement being permanent. But I don't want to hurt her."

"You'll have to tell her eventually," Kristie said.

"This *is* a nice place," Justin said as he surveyed the empty apartment.

"In an exciting city," Kristie said.

"And it's big enough for two," Justin said as he looked at Kristie.

"Call her," Kristie ordered.

*****

"He'll be home this evening about seven," Taylor said after she disconnected.

"Wednesday instead of Sunday, but good," Marty said.

"Yes. It will be good to have him home."

"Is he moving to Chicago?"

"He didn't say that he was. But I believe that he was holding something back."

Marty swallowed a lump in his throat and focused on his breath. "Well, then, I'll see you two this evening. Maybe he'll tell us then."

"See you this evening," Taylor said.

Marty hesitated for a moment in front of Justin and Taylor's door in order to quell the flutter in his chest. When he knocked, Taylor's voice rang out, "Come on in!" He opened the door and saw Taylor smile at him as she worked a corkscrew. Justin stood in the center of the room, next to a woman Marty didn't know.

"Hey bro," said Justin. "Guess what?"

The Sailing Quest

By Craig Ruark

The seconds were quickly counting down toward the three minute mark before the start of the race. Boat speed was building and position was crucial. The starting line was wide, about fifty yards across. "We're moving too fast," shouted Charlie in a tone of urgency. Without a word, Debbie quickly let the sail out, perhaps only six inches, but enough to spill off some wind that slows the boat down by half a knot. Then suddenly, a voice, piercingly loud, drew their attention. "*STARBOARD!*" shouted the captain on an approaching vessel. "*STARBOARD!*" He shouted again as his bow drew dangerously close. With scarcely time to react, Captain Charlie ordered a tack; you could hear the loud flapping of the jib as it moved across the bow and then the fast clicking of the gears in the winch as First Mate Debbie quickly pulled in the jib sheet as they maneuvered *Mariah*, out of the path of the approaching vessel.

They had avoided a collision, but that little maneuver put Mariah over the starting line and they would face a penalty if they did not make it back behind the line before the official start of the race. Charlie and Debbie scrambled to adjust their course and sails in order to build enough speed that would allow them to maneuver back across the starting line.

With just a minute left, Mariah was once again back in position for a clean start. Closer and closer they came to the invisible line as the crew of two watched the seconds count down on their start clock. They could see that the rest of the fleet was bearing down on them, each boat taking their own approach to the start of this race. Debbie started calling out the seconds, ten, five, four, three, two, one, and there it was... the sound of the horn... the race was on.

It was late October and the air was brisk for this 7 am start, but neither Captain Charlie nor First Mate Debbie could feel the chill beneath the adrenalin rush. The water showed scarcely a ripple from the eight knot breeze that was blowing from the shores of Lake Mead's Hemennway Beach. The sun had risen only a few degrees above the mountains that surrounded the lake, and it was expected that the breeze would build as the morning sun became more intense, heating up the rocky shores.

Mariah was one of over a dozen sailboats of various designs and sizes entered in a two-day race that would take them from the Boulder Basin, through the unforgiving "Narrows" to the Virgin Basin and Temple Bar Marina, some thirty miles and the finish on day one.

But eight knots of wind was light and did not leave much room for error as the Charlie and Debbie mate worked in unison setting the course and trimming the sails. Turning the boat had to be quick, smooth, and gentle in order to maintain speed.

As Debbie tightened up the sails, Charlie adjusted the course and Mariah picked up speed. It was eleven miles across Boulder Basin to the narrows. In sailing terms, that distance is converted to about 9.5 nautical miles. Top speed for Mariah was about six knots per hour, so in theory it would take about an hour and a half to cross this first watery divide. However, sailboats do not sail in straight lines, they must tack (change course), according to the direction of the wind, and so Charlie and Debbie settled back for a long morning sail. As they did, Charlie started thinking back to how they got to this point in their life.

This was Charlie and Debbie's second year as "official" boat owners; but it was the realization of a quest that had started some ten years earlier. The place was Austin, Texas, the year... 1984, and there it was, sitting on top a mountainous display of Coca-Cola soft drink cans inside the local grocery store, a red-hulled, twelve-foot, sailboat, sporting a little white sail with a red stripe emblazoned with Coca-Cola. At the base of the display was box with a slot in the top and a pad of official entry forms. Charlie quickly filled out one of the forms and stuffed it into the box. The next day he returned to fill out another form, and decided to take a few extra to fill out later. Soon, Charlie had stacks of forms that he had filled out and even more that his mother had filled out for him. There happened to be several stores in this grocery chain within a reasonable driving distance, and each one would have their own drawing. So to increase his chances, Charlie began distributing entries into four different store locations. By the day of the drawings, each of the entry boxes in three of the closest stores held several hundred of Charlie's contest entries; surely one of the boats would become his. The entry box at a fourth grocery location, a little off Charlie's usual beaten path, held just ten entry forms, the result of a whimsical trip to that part of town the night before the drawings.

Charlie's office was in the basement of his parent's home, where he and his father operated a family-owned consulting firm. On the day of the sailboat drawings, Debbie, his mother and the rest of the family stood clustered around his desk. Charlie picked up the telephone and dialed the store closest to his office, and the one that held the most entries; nearly nine-hundred. When the person on the other end of the line answered, Charlie excitedly asked if the drawing for the sailboat had been held. When the voice answered yes, his excitement grew even more, but when the winning name was announced it wasn't him, and the room was silent.

Just as quickly as he hung up the receiver, Charlie began dialing the second store. Chances of winning were still good at this location with nearly five hundred entries in the box. But alas, when the person answered, Charlie's name would not be the one he heard.

Ahhh, but there is the third store; and although it's contest box only contained two hundred or less entries, Charlie hoped that the odds were still in his favor. There is an old saying, "Third time is a charm" but it would not hold true for Charlie. If each of those entries had been real money on a table in Vegas, he would be going home with empty pockets.

Feeing defeated, but knowing that he had to make the call, Charlie began dialing the fourth store who's entry box contained ten forms with his name. A voice answered and Charlie calmly asked about their drawing. "Well," said the voice on the other end, "our manager was not working today so the drawing won't be held until tomorrow."

The next day, Charlie was busy at his desk when his mother & Debbie brought lunch down for him and his father. "Did you call about the drawing?" they asked. "No, but I will call right now." He replied, as he nonchalantly picked-up the receiver and began to dial.

"Hello," he said, "I am calling to find out if you have held the drawing for the sailboat."

"Great, can you tell me the name of the winner?"

"Who?"

"Can you spell the name?"

"That's me! When can I pick it up?"

"I'll be right over."

As he hung up the phone, everyone in the room thought that he was putting them on and didn't believe the conversation. "Come on", he said, "let's go claim my boat." There was continued laughter as if they were all being lead on. "We'll need to take some rope and mom's Buick; it will be large enough to carry the boat on the roof." With that, Charlie sprang from his desk and started for the garage to gather the rope, "I'll meet you at the car."

Along for the ride, but still not believing that he had actually won the sailboat, Debbie and his mother were shocked when they walked through the front door of the grocery. There it was, sitting atop a freezer full of Ice, and a sign taped to the side was the boat. It was indeed Charlie's name printed in bold letters.

The boat was light and was easily transported back to Charlie's parents, and he could hardly wait for the weekend when he could launch his magnificent "ship" on Town Lake in downtown Austin…

Mariah was approaching the "Narrows" and interrupted his little daydream. The tiny gorge is about a mile long and no more than twenty-five yards wide in places. They would be sailing against the current and the dominant wind direction which meant constantly tacking back and forth across the gorge sometimes advancing only a few yards at a time. Charlie held one hand on the tiller while the other controlled the main sheet. When they tacked, Charlie would release the main slightly to allow it to flip to the opposite tack. Debbie controlled the Jib which she would release from a winch on one side of the boat and just as quickly crank on the opposite winch to bring to sail to the other side of the boat. This ballet of sorts, took tremendous timing and was a lot of work for a two person crew. Their precision on this day was flawless, but to an onlooker, each tack would appear to be as chaotic as a "Chinese Fire Drill" One-hundred-nine tacks later, both Charlie and Debbie were exhausted but they had made it through the Narrows and back to open water. They were now in the Virgin Basin section of Lake Mead, and about 20 miles to the finish of the first leg of the race.

As they set course for Temple Bar Marina, it was time for a little lunch and a well-deserved relaxing sail. Charlie could not help but think back to his first sail. Town Lake was actually the Little Colorado River that was dammed up on the east and west side of town creating a narrow body of fairly deep water that separated the northern and southern parts of town. Like the narrows, Town Lake for the most part was only a few hundred yards wide but instead of rocky canyon walls, it had a beautiful tree lined shore.

Charlie remembered being so eager to try out his new sailboat. The instruction manual was the equivalent of four double-sided, letter size pieces of paper: with a cover, three pages that contained a parts list and instructions for rigging the boat, three pages of sailing instructions with large diagrams, and a back cover. Charlie quickly scanned the pages, assembled the sail to the mast and boom and placed the mast in a holder near the bow of the boat. Next the rudder was attached to the tiller and placed in a bracket at the stern. A little center board slipped into a compartment in the bottom of the boat and she was ready to sail. A couple of flotation cushions were placed for comfort and safety on the wood seat that ran from side to side.

Charlie held the boat to the shore and motioned for Debbie to climb aboard. "No Way" she exclaimed, "first you go out and sail around in a circle three times and then back to shore, to prove that you can sail this thing, then I will THINK about getting in."

With that, Charlie launched from the shore and sailed out to the middle of the river. He performed his first tack and then another and another, each time a little bit better than the time before. After performing his maneuvers', he sailed back to shore, and Debbie mustered enough courage to climb aboard.

A few years later, Charlie left Austin, for a business venture in Camden, Maine; he took his twelve-foot sailboat with him. During the summer he would spend weekends in Camden Harbor, where hundreds of sailboats would sit at anchor. These boats looked massive, long and sleek with bright polished chrome and shiny teak. Their masts seem to reach right up to the sun and when one would sail out the harbor their sails would glisten, bright white against the blue sky. Those yachts must be worth a million bucks; Charlie thought to himself as he skimmed the water in his twelve-foot, Styrofoam and plastic *Snark*.

Once again Charlie's thoughts were interrupted as Mariah was nearly across the Virgin Basin; the finish line for the first leg was in site. Charlie and Debbie easily tacked their way across the finish and dropped the sails in preparation for docking.

That evening there was drinking and laughter and many stories shared about the day's sail. Charlie and Debbie had been racing for two years since they bought Mariah. It was a learning experience, teaching them how to manipulate the boat from point A to point B in the most precise manner. To date, they had never finished closer than fifth place in any race. However, earlier that summer, they had hauled the boat out of the water, and working side by side for three weekends, scraped several layers of calcium build-up off the hull of the boat, sanded it smooth and put on two coats of a very thin racing paint that would help prevent future growth. They felt good about their performance in today's sail.

After dinner, Charlie and Debbie went down below deck for a good night's sleep. But sleep did not last very long. Around 1 am, the winds started picking up and Mariah was being rocked violently against the dock. Charlie went on deck to make sure the rubber fenders were securely fastened to the boat, and secure the dock lines; he didn't want a hole rubbed through the fiberglass hull by the wooden dock.

Five in the morning came quite early as Charlie and Debbie rolled out of their bunk, to prepare for the day's sail. It was dark and the air was quite brisk, made even colder by a persistent twenty-knot wind.

After breakfast, and afraid that the heavy winds and gusts might be too much for the light weight 175 sq ft jib sail, Charlie replaced it with a much smaller and heavier 135 sq ft jib. As they left the dock, Charlie also put a double reef in the mainsail to decrease the amount of cloth.

The minutes and seconds clicked down toward the start of this morning's leg and Mariah was off to a smooth start. It would take a number of tacks to get through the narrow starting area and out to the open water of the Virgin Basin. Little did they know that things were about to get a little rough.

Mounted at the top of the mast was a wind indicator, and as Charlie looked up to get a fix on the wind direction, he noticed that the top quarter of the mast was bending slightly to starboard under the pressure of the sail against the wind. The port side upper shroud (the wire cable that held the mast in place), was too slack for the wind conditions and needed to be tightened before they lost the mast completely. Quickly, Charlie gave the command for a tack to release the pressure on the shroud so that it could be adjusted

At the base of the shroud was a turnbuckle that connected the cable to the deck and allowed for tension adjustments. Because of the heavy wind, it was difficult for Debbie to hold the tiller, so it was up to her to put a few turns on the turnbuckle to tighten the shroud. As she reached down toward the deck a gust of wind buried the railing in the water, along with Debbie's feet up to her ankles. With one hand holding tightly to the wood railing atop the cabin, Debbie reached over with her other hand to twist the turnbuckle; unfortunately, as a lefty, she turned the wrong direction and the turnbuckle parted from the deck bolt. They were in trouble. "You must re-thread the turnbuckle back onto the bolt." shouted Charlie, trying to make his voice heard above the sound of the wind and the waves. "Just a few turns so that it makes a good connection." he continued to shout..."But hurry, we don't have much time, we are approaching some rocks and must tack."

Debbie was unaware of the approaching shoreline and became even more nervous about her task. In order to reconnect the turnbuckle, she would need both hands which meant that she had to release her grip on the hand rail. She quickly crouched down, one knee on the deck, grabbed the lower bolt with her right hand and threaded the turnbuckle on with her left hand. She only had time to put about six turns on the turnbuckle before heading back to the cockpit to prepare for a tack.

"Tacking," shouted Charlie, not waiting for the standard reply of "Ready" from his first mate, as he quickly pushed the tiller toward the port side of the boat, bringing the bow across to starboard. Simultaneously, Debbie released the port side jib sheet and just as quickly began hauling in the slack on the starboard jib sheet. Charlie, looked back to see the rocky coast moving away from their little boat. But they still had a problem; the top of the mast was bending even further.

"We can't stay on this tack very long, the mast can't take this… we need to tighten that shroud" Charlie said, looking for acknowledgement from Debbie. Charlie could sense that Debbie did not want go forward again. "Listen," Charlie took Debbie's hand, "you take the helm after we tack and I will go forward to tighten the shroud…I'll make it quick and be back before you know it, we have to do this." Debbie looked over Charlie's shoulder and could see that they had made good distance away from the rocks, "Ok" she said and prepared for the tack. "Tacking," Charlie called out and pushed the tiller to starboard. Again, with precision and speed, Debbie released the starboard jib sheet and began pulling the port side jib sheet. You could hear the whirring of gears of the winch as the ropes made the drum spin. Once the jib was hauled in, she looped the ends of the sheets around the deck cleats with a half twist on the final turn to lock them in place; and then positioned herself to take control of the tiller.

As Charlie moved forward onto the deck, the weight of his body made the rail of the boat dip even further under water. As he kneeled down to grab the turnbuckle he recited an old rhyme to himself…Lefty Loosey…Righty Tighty…and confirmed in his head that he must turn the buckle to the right. As promised, he made quick work of the job and returned the cockpit to relieve Debbie of the helm. "That should be good for now," he stated, "lets prepare to tack and get away from those rocks for good." "Aye aye Captain." Debbie quipped with a wink and a smile, "Ready to tack."

After Charlie and Debbie completed the tack, they sat back to take a bit of a breather. It was the first time since the start of the race that they had a chance to survey the rest of the fleet. A few of the larger faster boats were a head of them already making their way across the Virgin Basin toward the Narrows. But they were surprised to see a good number of boats still behind them. One more tack and they too were now into the open water of the basin. The winds were beginning to calm a bit and although the mast was not perfectly straight, they were not in any danger.

The sail across the Virgin Basin was long and the wind dropped off to more of a breeze. Charlie locked the tiller in place and went forward to shake the reefs out of the mainsail and hoist it to the top of the mast. He thought about changing the Jib for one a little larger and lighter, but they were already close to their top speed of six knots.

After a few hours they were approaching the Narrows and by then the wind had nearly completely died and up ahead they could see the committee boat and hear the sound of an air horn marking the finish as each boat passed. Because of the lack of wind, the race committee decided to shorten the course to just before the Narrows.

As Mariah crossed the invisible finish line, they received their acknowledgement from the race official. But it was still some fifteen miles back to the marina. Charlie reached over the stern of the boat and adjusted the bracket that dropped the little six horse power *Evinrude* motor into running position, set the choke, gave couple of squeezes on the fuel bulb to prime the engine, and gave a strong pull on the starter rope. The little engine sputtered at first and then started to catch as Charlie slowly backed off the choke. In a matter of seconds, the *Evinrude* was propelling the boat forward. Charlie moved swiftly to the bow of the boat as Debbie released the jib halyard from the cleat and began lowering the sail. As the cloth came down, Charlie gathered it on the deck and secured it with bungee cord to prevent it from falling overboard. The two then brought down the main sail, flaking the folds in an alternating pattern port and starboard then secured it to the boom with nylon straps.

With the sails secure, the two relaxed in the cockpit, cocktail in hand taking in the beauty of this watery oasis surrounded by desert mountains.

By the time Mariah had reached its slip, the sails and gear had been properly stowed, and boat was in shipshape condition. Charlie and Debbie quickly made their way to the marina patio for the after race party. After all the crews had arrived, and before the liquor took over the evening, the race committee sounded the air horn to get everyone's attention. It was time to announce the race results.

The winner of a sailboat race is determined through a series of calculations that include the standard racing handicap given to each model boat and the time it took for each boat to complete the course. Given their past performance, Charlie and Debbie were only half listening as the results' in each class were announced starting with third place and working their way up to the winning boats. "And FIRST PLACE, in the non-spinnaker class... MARIAH!"

Charlie was dazed and thoughts rambled through his head, back to those days aboard that tiny twelve foot *Snark* with the Coca Cola Sail, in Camden Harbor, and suddenly those mega sailing yachts paled in beauty when compared to *Mariah*. Charlie and Debbie had achieved their quest.

Hot Springs

By M. McCutcheon

I took a cold shower and wondered at what we'd done. We were home and somehow found our way back. My weathered face and wrecked hair will still there after the shower. I sat down to reflect about this journey in Nevada.

I had eaten some suspicious red bell peppers in my life, the ones that had curly, bulbous growths on the inside, when others did not. I wonder still if they, or something like them, are the cause of my disease.

So my love and I decided to go in search of a healthful healing place. We knew green trees places were good, and negative ion places such as waterfalls too. I chose to go to hot springs in Nevada, anywhere in Nevada.

Our first spring was Bog Hot Creek in Northwestern Nevada. We drove north from Henderson to Winnemucca and stayed overnight in a gas station. It was a beautiful drive full of mountain views and we saw a lot of big horn sheep, one even got stuck on our bumper.

I neglected to check the temperature and even though it was August, I suffered a burn injury when I put my leg into that gorgeous sanctuary pond. I screamed and my honey went and got ice from the cooler. The darn natural spring was just too damn hot.

On our outward stop, the gas station guy in Denio said that there was a man found floating there. He most likely dove in and cooked like a lobster.

I bought a thermometer at the Ace Hardware store as we headed to Gerlach. It was possibly for cooking or outdoor/indoor measurement. It was nice and long so that I could dip deeper than under a tongue for hotness.

Gerlach was where Soldier Meadows Hot Spring was, well, it was 62 miles north. It was incredibly beautiful! There was a pool of water and it was surrounded by reeds. No one else was there – it is important to honor "hot spring étiquette"– such as if someone else was there, such as a couple...such as a naked couple...the party coming should go away for awhile. Privacy and reverence for nature and love-making and that sort of thing.

Then, oh Lordy, Lordy...a couple snaked out by the reeds and they were naked. The woman had her arm around the man's neck and they swooned into vision. I stalled for a moment, then looked for their vehicle of high desert transportation. They must have walked in and put their stuff outside the bushes.

My darling captured my hand that wasn't holding the thermometer and led me back to our vehicle. It was nearing noon that day and we had to either wait or go. My thermometer said the pool was approximately 94 degrees. I chose to wait. We looked at each other and admired too, the beauty of Nevada. It was so nice being here in the sand and scrub. My love left me no envy for the couple in the pool, I floated higher I think. We then left, they never did.

No need to stop at a truck stop this time but headed to the Geysers, just 20 miles north of Gerlach. I couldn't believe my eyes! Shooting spray of hot geothermal water.

My thermometer read 104 degrees. It was too hot for me, but worth the trip. We had to walk a bit to find it, but it was a fountain of youth or health and just what I was looking for.

However, I was walking barefoot along the path and damn it hurt, I hit my left 3rd toe on a tree root. Again my love came to my side and simply held me in his arms, as we looked at my distraught toe. It was stiff and secure among its brethren, so we got up and walked along. It was no fault of nature or the owner of the land, it simply happened. I went and soaked my foot in a glorious pool that was cool enough. All these geysers were shooting up too, but my toe which turned blue and thick took precedence.

We decided to go south and by a beautiful sunset we found Steamboat Hot Springs. The water was still shooting out of the spring at over 300 degrees. It was amazing to see, and the private rooms of tubs were incredibly lovely, fresh shower and we wished they had a hotel room. We soaked in the one little outdoor tub and wondered why they didn't have ten little outdoor tubs. The rules of etiquette had no place here. A big hairy sweaty man you'd never met could come right next to you. This hot spring place has a belief of just being as it is, no changes. We all soak together.

To Reno, and then to Pyramid Lake Hot Spring. We stayed at a nice casino for a cheap price. The water there was wonderful too. We flew some golf balls into a lake at their nice driving range and boated out of there. My incredible man caught an 8 lb. cut-throat trout on the lake and then we endured a huge exciting storm. Our car actually moved while we waited it out. I started to feel stronger all the time. This spring was located on a Paiute Indian land, we were glad to pay any fee and there was a revered pyramid shaped rock in the lake, which is off limits, but we were happy to see. I never used the thermometer.

We skipped Blossom Hot Pot earlier and now were skipping everything around Carson to get to the south. We decided to lay down a blanket near Crystal Warm Springs, 103 miles north of Las Vegas. My sweetheart was fooling around with trout and I ran like a maniac. There were ground bees right near our blanket, a hole with beautiful bumble bees. We packed up and left. I began to want for bakers and pastries and smooth coffee. Yet we headed for Warm Springs at Moapa. I moped and smeared my nose on the window toward the beautiful desert sky and mountains. My darling likes to smear his snout all over my body and I love it. I broke my thermometer and we ran away.

We found the cheapest motel and it was cheap. No towels, no soap, and I didn't trust the sheets, but they looked clean and inviting. No bugs were on the walls and there was a window that could be opened.

We drove and got to the town of Panaca. We learned the springs here were part of a domestic venture by Brigham Young. It is a place he chose to run to, if being chased from Utah. The hot spring happened to be drained, they open flood gates once a year and release the water. Wonderful pools and a splendid day with my gorgeous guy, I trusted the guy and the water temperature were what I hoped for.

My body felt better but my mind began to wonder. What truth is there in these mystical warm hot springs that come from deep in our earth? We came home to Henderson and I felt so much better. We made a plan to go east. Ash Hot Springs are on BLM land and we gladly paid the fee to sit in the concrete pool. It was a gorgeous nature refuge. Then at sunset, some traveler brought a Conure parrot and it escaped from their camper. I was no longer the highest rated maniac in camper land. The bird flew around and around and landed on the lowest level head, which was my love, as he rested in the pool next to me. I admired the deep green feathers and the determined look that was in the bird's eye. The distressed captor of the bird came and put out her finger as my sweetie and I set in the warm water. The bird alighted to her hand

and was simply praised.

Is there some message that comes with all these hot spring waters? We decided next to avoid Caliente Hot Springs because we had too much hot of hot springs. We went anyway, they have private tubs and cold water too. 42 miles east of 375 and 93, it is a motel with plumbing from the spring. Next thing I know some girl shows up to bring and extra towel. Then, some guy shows up with a tray of extra drinks at reasonable prices. Water for free. I'd hate some towels but love some extra water and then there was a huge fray. We were thrown out and stay at the T&Y truck stop.

There is nothing more beautiful in Nevada than the man that I love. The sun rise came and so did I. I felt so good. Heading to Roger's Hot Spring today! We tried to go to a place that is actually very sacred land, permission was not granted and big grey horse snoots asked why we were there. I could only back away in the warm soft water. We met Chris somebody? who wrote the gate to hell song, he was trying to find heaven too. The spring was not open.

So the next Spring we tried was Rogers Warm Spring, 16 miles south of Overton. It is near Lake Mead and the temperature fluctuates.. we headed toward the Valley of Fire and I don't know what happened. My love saw a powered para-glider and stopped the car.

Then, the bird flew out and we couldn't catch her, then the dog went nuts and ran away across the dry desert lake.

There is a warm spring that comes by faucet in our

country. Not everyone has it but it is usually revered for its unique mineral and soaking quality. In Nevada, we live a beautiful majority. Many, many beautiful and exciting places to lose ones bird or find a new dog.

So home in the cool shower, I washed off little pieces of weeds from my hair. I rinsed off a blister that used to be a callus from my toe. I wanted for a wash tub of health and a soak for beauty and everlasting life. My tears were saltier than any ocean water. My waves were nearly as severe as those that crash with the storms on water. I am going to die in Nevada. I just don't know it yet.

I try to better my health. We plan the next journey to Ash Springs. Then we change our mind to drive all the way to Silver Peak Hot Spring. We got in the car and drove to Tonopah. There was one nice hotel. They had an old bearing, having been built in the 1800's. Old for the United States but not for Europe or Asia. Yet, there was a ghost. I did not expect to meet the other side like this, but a lady came and slept with my man.

She is known to roam the house and seduce men at night. Especially in Room Number 12 for some reason. I understand a man whom she dearly loved came by, and said he was going to the hot spring and to snare hares and would be back. He never returned and his body was floating in a too hot pool. She never learned of that.

So we had a visit from her and may have been near the waters of him. I do not want to ever wake up weary wonder about people who do. We are packing and boarding and heading to Metropolis, then Ruby Valley Hot Spring in northern Nevada, even though we live and love in the south east near the Henderson airport with a dog and a bird.

We made love at the mountains near Tonopah, the place was peaceful and the air was like breathing a fresh made pastry by a master chef.

And I died happy.

Finding Billyniceguy

By Barbra Wolfe

My name is Amanda Weyling, and today I'm conducting my fourth of six online dating interviews for the *Nevada Lifestyle* Channel. The network powers-that-be decided to segment internet dating by age brackets as if the motivations for looking for Mr. Right vary solely by age. That is so not the case but what the heck; I'm just a reporter and I need this job.

The topic today is *New Love After 50* and I'm here in Summerlin, a lovely planned community west of Las Vegas, at the home of Melanie Jenn. My fact sheet states that she's fifty-six, divorced, and has explored online dating. I checked her out on Facebook, and from her posts and laughing blue eyes, she looks like a hoot and a half.

Ah! Here she comes now with our hair and make-up artists in tow. She's dressed smart casual: khakis, navy blouse, and stylish high-heeled sandals. Judging from her shoes, I'll bet she has a room just for shoes.

"Good morning Ms. Jenn. I'm Amanda Weyling and I am so happy to meet you," I say as I extend my hand. "Thank you so much for agreeing to do this interview."

"Good morning, it's my pleasure." She gives me a firm handshake.

"I think everyone is ready on your patio. We just need to get this wireless microphone hooked on, and then you'll be ready too. The whole interview shouldn't take more than half an hour."

We stroll outside onto a charming lattice covered patio decked with all sorts of potted flowers. Beyond that is a beautiful desert landscaped garden filled with trees, bushes and cacti in bloom. There's a dirt walking path that begins at one end of the patio, winds around a raised island, and ends at the cement path on the far side of the house. I've lived in Vegas all my life and I've never seen a backyard as lovely as this. It's like a mini park. "Oh, this is beautiful," I say.

"Thanks!" she replies, with an ear-to-ear smile.

Birds chirp nearby while a slight breeze and a pleasant fragrance caress the air. I can hear children splashing and laughing faintly in the distance. I find myself very relaxed.

Laney, our director and lighting guru, is busy examining a tiered planter in the shape of a shoe. What did I tell you? I knew Melanie was into shoes.

I introduce Melanie to Todd, the lead cameramen. Todd explains the different angles they plan to shoot and which camera she should always look at when she's not looking at me.

We sit at the main table. Olivia, the make-up artist, sits with the hair stylist at one of three conversational seating areas strategically placed along the walking path.

The cameras roll as we begin.

"So, Melanie... may I call you Melanie?"

"Yes, of course. Actually, Mel is fine," replies the cheery-faced woman who is clearly going to be a pleasure to work with.

"Okay Mel, our audience wants to know about your quest for finding love after fifty."

"I'd be happy to share that, Amanda, but in all honesty, my quest started way before I was fifty."

"Well, why don't you start with when you decided to try internet dating," I say, smiling at her and then the camera. "What prompted you?"

"Well," she starts, "meeting normal, nice, available, straight guys in Vegas is not that easy at fifty-six. A couple of my friends had tried online dating and were successful, so I thought I'd give it a shot."

"So, you just dove in?"

"Oh no, I had some homework to do first."

"Like what?" None of my previous interviewees had mentioned homework, so my interest is piqued.

Pushing her bangs to the side, she continues, "Well, I had always heard that in order to manifest what you want you really have to have a clear picture of what it is that you actually desire. So, eventually I made a list of everything I wished for in my ideal partner and that's when my quest for happiness, balance and love began."

"I'm going to remember that," I say, writing a note to myself on the back of one of my handy blue index cards. "I've not yet tried online dating myself. Actually, before doing this series, I found the idea of it a little daunting. Were you at all leery?"

"Once I had made the decision, I was on board 100%. It was scary in the beginning, but as my mamma used to say, 'nothing ventured, nothing gained'."

"How open were you?"

She takes a sip of water and sweeps her arms dramatically in an outward circling motion. "As I wrote my profile, I decided to put myself out there. I wasn't doing this to play games. I wanted to be authentic and sum myself up so they could get to know me quickly. And I came right out with what I was looking for in a man. I figured they didn't know me from a hole in the wall so what did I have to lose, right?"

"Like a grocery list?" I ask this because the woman representing our 30 to 39 year old segment had a laundry list that rivaled a child's list to Santa.

"No, but I've heard there are women who actually publish lists of what they don't want. Mine was conversational and included only the positives. The things I didn't want in a guy were part of the initial screening that I kept to myself."

"Ah hah," I say, leaning over to her in a conspiratorial manner. "So tell us, what would immediately disqualify someone?"

"I want to say first that there is nothing bad about any of these attributes. They just weren't a good fit for me."

"Okay, understood," I say nodding my head in agreement.

"I'm spiritual, but not religious, so if a guy indicated that religion was very important to him, he was ruled out."

"So I'm guessing you didn't use one of those religious dating sites?"

"You are correct on that assumption. And if someone was super conservative to the point of being in love with Sarah Palin, he was tossed out the window in a New York second."

"I like it. You've covered religion and politics right off the bat. What else?"

"Lots of tattoos or photos of him with his motorcycle were a big turnoff. I also excluded short guys and anyone who seemed overboard on exercise and sports."

"Okay, now we know what you're not into," I josh. "You haven't mentioned age. Were you looking for a sugar daddy or were you planning to be a cougar?"

Mel laughs. "Great question! Actually, I was looking for roughly my age, give or take a few years."

"Okay, anything else?"

She tilts her head and looks up to the right. "Yes," she says, nodding. Then looking at me, she continues. "If his favorite things to do were camping and hunting, then we were not a good match. Oh, and teeth! Teeth were another factor. If I didn't see teeth in the photos, I assumed there might be some missing."

"Oh my God, that's so funny about the teeth. You are the first one to mention that and you're right. If they smiled with their lips closed, or they didn't smile at all, you wouldn't know, would you?"

Although it's cool out, tiny beads of perspiration have already formed on her eyebrows and upper lip. I wonder if it's her nerves or a hot flash causing this.

"Cut!" yells Laney.

I reassure Mel that everything is going great. "I just want to take a second to powder your face. Also, do you have the list of characteristics you wanted in your ideal guy?"

"No, but I have the profile I published on the dating sites. Do you want me to get it?"

"Yes, if it's not too much trouble. I think that would definitely be of interest to our viewers. We'll take five."

While Mel is inside, I walk over to Olivia, who is sitting comfortably under the shade of a tree, and ask her to work her magic on Mel when she returns.

A few minutes later, Mel comes back with a printout of her profile and Olivia quickly applies some makeup. We're ready to resume.

"Mel, please share with us what you wrote about your perfect man."

"Sure Amanda. My headline read: Looking for the one who will make my heart sing just by being him."

"Oh, I love that." I coo.

"Oh here we go," she says, pointing at a sentence on her paper. "I am looking for a man who is loving, caring and kind, loves movies, barbequing at home as much as dining out, and enjoys the performing arts (or will at least go with me occasionally just for my sake). My ideal man is as comfortable attending a charity or business dinner as he is hanging out in jeans, confidant, financially and emotionally secure, and preferably an incurable romantic to help curb my slight workaholic tendencies."

"Well that's concise and to the point."

"I don't think I was asking for too much," she says, shrugging.

Just then she pauses as a hummingbird hovers by her ear. She doesn't move a muscle until it flies away.

"Are they the coolest birds ever?" she asks rhetorically.

"Very cool. I've never seen them come that close before," I reply.

"Oh, they beat their wings in my ears all the time. They love my garden."

"So, you were reading," I prompt. "Was that the end or is there more?"

"Oh, there's more," she says looking at her bio. "Blah, blah, blah, oh, here's the kicker." She resumes reading out loud. "Life is good and I'm in a good place. The only thing missing is that special someone who can be my best friend and make me feel like I'm sixteen again with a fifty-six year old brain; someone who is both tender and passionate and who gets me as much as I get him. I'm looking for someone with whom I can grow and possibly grow old with. Building a life together will be an incredible journey. And.... it's all about the journey."

"That was beautiful," I comment, pushing some loose hair behind my right ear. "I love the journey line, because it *is* all about the journey, isn't it? Wow! So which sites did you use? We know you didn't use any of the religious ones."

"Right you are. I didn't use any of the senior sites either. I don't want to advertise, so let's just say that I used two of the more popular ones."

"Okay," I say to the audience, "that narrows it down."

Referring to my index cards, I ask, "Mel, how hard was it to find men who met your expectations?"

"It wasn't easy. Actually my quest started out a bit bumpy."

"How so?"

"I set up a separate email account using my fake on-line name and was bombarded by weirdos, hornies, con artists, and an overall colorful bunch of fellas. And, I learned that self-employed often meant unemployed."

"Con artists?" I ask. "Care to delve into that a bit?"

"My first online relationship lasted three weeks. He

was a con artist. Thanks to him and several others, I now know how to spot one a mile away. Actually, may I give your audience a heads up on what to look out for in general?"

"Sure. I think we'd all appreciate that."

She sits up straight and looks directly into the camera. Her smile is gone and her face has an intense look about it.

"Okay. If he tells you his entire life story in the first few emails and has a heartbreaking story about his wife or kids, be wary."

She's very serious and actually pointing at the camera. Note to self, we may want to cut this later.

She continues, "If he doesn't live in your immediate vicinity, be careful. If he gives you his personal email address to avoid being on the public site, be cautious. If he spells out "dotcom" in his email address, don't go any further. If he has relocated from another country make sure your antennae are on full alert."

I notice that my skirt has ridden up a little too high on my thigh. I give it a little tug before asking, "Why, did you encounter foreigners?"

"Yes, I did. Besides the British widower con artist in Reno, I interacted with a New Zealand widower with two children in Laughlin, a Norwegian divorcee in St. George, and a Bulgarian interior decorator on a job in Turkey who said he resided in New York and Florida."

"It seems like there are a lot of scammers online."

"There are. Oh! And one more thing," she warns, "if he

asks you right up front how long you've been online dating and what your experience has been, he's probably trying to find out if you know how to spot a con artist."

I laugh and attempt to change the flow of the conversation. "Well thank you for the tips. So did you have any non-con artist experiences before you met Mr. Right?"

"Yes I did. The weeding and probing for a 'nice guy'," she makes air quotation marks, "almost became a full time job."

"So how were you meeting these men? Emails? Texts? Phone? Dates?"

Mel starts laughing. It is clear that she's out of her lecture-to-protect mode and back into her story. "All of the above," she snorts mid laugh. She did not just snort on TV, did she? Please tell me she didn't snort.

"Among the most notable, in no particular order, were pool guy, insurance guy, I saw him for a month, wine club guy, and dancer guy."

She suddenly cracks up laughing. Covering her face with her hands, she moans, "Oh my God."

"Care to share?"

"Sorry! I'm just remembering insurance guy. He was very impressed with himself in more ways than one."

"Okay, I am not going there," I say, blushing and raising my hand to make her stop.

She continues, "Then there was pizza owner guy number one. Our first date was a concert at the Smith Center."

She is counting on her fingers now. "Then there was hippie hiker dude who showed up wearing a Civil War hat. It turns out he was a Confederate general in a previous life but had failed to mention that in his bio."

Mel is becoming very animated. She is visibly getting a kick out of herself as she dishes her dirt.

"Then there was pizza owner guy number two who, as it turned out, was not yet officially divorced and was obsessed with complaining about his wife. And I can't leave out massage therapist S&M guy." She rolls her eyes and laughingly says, "Oh my God, one walk in the park was enough of him."

She's on a roll and I've got a question. I wave my hands to interrupt and one of my blue index cards goings flying. "Okay Mel, I have to ask. What's with the pizza owner guys?"

She giggles and shakes her head no. "It was just a coincidence. I'll admit to being a pizza lover, a pizza snob actually, but I swear I didn't put that in my search criteria."

She uncrosses her legs and leans over to me. "I was looking for someone to make my heart sing just by being him and you know what? I eventually found him."

"How did you know?"

"Well to start with, his online persona was 'billyniceguy'. His profile picture was of him and one of his granddaughters, which I thought was sweet. That alone made his bio worth reading." She adjusts her glasses. "His intro read something like, 'My female friends are always saying that all the nice guys are taken. Well, I'm a nice guy.'

"So I read on. He said he liked to travel. YAY!" she says as she throws her arms in the air.

"He said he liked to play golf." She jumps in her seat. "Even better! I thought.

"He said he liked to play tennis. I can learn.

"And, not that he was an alcoholic, but he said, if the reader didn't drink, it wasn't going to work out. He had tried dating other women who didn't drink, and it didn't work. He said he liked to open a bottle of wine, turn on some music and then cook together."

And then with her Southern drawl she says, "At that point I thought to myself, "Oh my God, can this get any better?"

"Actually, I'm thinking the same thing. Go on."

"We started with emails and then moved on to phone calls," she continues. "He lived in Henderson and he owned his own solar energy business."

"He sounds so normal."

"That's what I said."

"So did you check him out like you did the scammer?"

"Of course I did. I checked out his Facebook page. I checked out his friends." She furrows her eyebrows and tilts her head as she thinks. "I remember coming to the conclusion that we had friends of friends in common, so chances were low that he was wanted for murder someplace. I Googled him and found his company's web-site. He appeared legit but still, I felt it best to meet him in a public place."

"That was smart. Where did you meet?"

"Our first date was set for a Thursday night at Brio in Town Square."

"Did he look like his picture? I've heard some horror stories about guys posting fake pictures."

"Yes, I recognized him right away. He was sitting on the patio with a bottle of Chardonnay. We talked for a long time and got to know each other. He asked questions off the top of his head. I asked questions from my notebook. Yesssss," she says drawing out the word yes, "I brought a notebook with a list of questions and made no effort to hide it." She giggles. "He thought it was pretty funny."

"Sounds like you're a list person."

"I am! And guess what? So is he. We totally hit it off and wound up joining his friends over at Tommy Bahama's bar. When we left, he walked me to my car and Wow!" she says, rolling her head, "He was a great kisser. I remember whispering, 'I feel like I've known you all my life'."

I look straight at Todd's camera and say, "Now we're getting to the good part."

Addressing Mel, I ask, "So did you take it slow or start seeing each other a lot right away?"

"Well, we met Saturday at Sedona, over on Flamingo. One thing led to another and let's just say that the next morning the front door was still ajar. Luckily, my dog had not escaped. My purse was on the floor near the door. Fortunately, I had not been robbed. My jacket was on the floor in the hallway to the bedroom where, with skill, he had taken me to a place few men ever have."

She pauses and her mouth hangs open for a second too long. She is beet red having realized what she's just told millions of people on TV. She swallows hard. "I forgot the question; did I answer it?" she asks meekly.

"Yes, I would say so," I joke. Adjusting my sitting position, I cross my legs and lean to the side, away from Mel, giving her center stage. I gesture with my hands. "Please go on."

"That Sunday," she resumes, "I went to see his office and his house.

"The following Friday we went to the movies at Red Rock followed by drinks on the outside patio at T-Bones. It was a perfect night, the weather was gorgeous, the atmosphere romantic. Just as we were leaving, a few women sitting nearby called over to us and shared that they couldn't wait to get home to their significant others after seeing us together. I have to say that I was happy."

"Mel, this is so romantic."

Shaking her head in agreement and leaning over to me, she says, "It was! By the second date, we were already finishing each other's sentences and literally thinking the same thoughts. By the fourth date, he showed up in an outfit that was an identical men's version of mine. We were so in sync it might have been creepy if it wasn't so adorable."

She starts laughing. It gets more intense. She's remembering something funny. She's holding her tummy and rolls forward in her chair. When she raises her head back up she is laughing hysterically; tears are running down her cheeks. She tries to speak but can't get the words out. She slaps the table. Oh crap, she just drooled on the table. The guys are going to have a blast with this in the editing room.

I don't know what she's laughing at, but it's contagious and now I'm laughing too. As a matter of fact, the entire crew is cracking up. Two minutes go by. I've lost control of the interview; thank God we're not live. I have no idea if the cameras are even still rolling. Another minute goes by and Mel begins to compose herself. Olivia, ever at the ready, hands her a wad of tissues. I grab one too and dab below my eyes.

"Are you okay? Do we need to break?" I ask this sincerely as she is clearly red in the face.

"I'm so sorry. Sometimes I start laughing and I just can't stop!" she says drying her face. I hope she didn't pee her pants. "When Billy is with me and this happens, he reminds me to breathe. Seriously, he'll shout 'BREATHE, MEL, BREATHE!'

"Oh, I'm not sure where I was. Oh yeah." she says, as she sits up taller and gives one final dab to her right eye. She is much more serious when she continues. "Then I found out that a friend of mine knew him. I remember she bubbled, 'Oh my God, Steve and I love him!'"

Laney gives me a hand signal. I've got five minutes to

wrap this up.

"That must have put your mind at ease."

"Honestly, I was glad for some third party validation," she concurs. "This all seemed too good to be true. I was kind of waiting for the other shoe to drop, you know?"

I nod, roll my eyes and reply, "I know exactly what you mean."

"A psychic told me that this was the third time that Billy and I had been together. That's rare enough, but even more so was that we were in romantic relationships in each of those lifetimes."

We're going a little off course here, but I'm curious. "Did you believe her?"

"Well, I didn't know how much to believe, but I had been told in the past by others that when I met 'the one', I'd know it. It would feel like I'd known him forever."

"So do you think you found your soul mate?"

"Oh, who knows? I'd like to think so." She smiles. "It's been a year since we met. I've never known a more considerate, loving man in my life. He loves me and I love him."

Dreamy eyed, she continues, "It was well worth the wait. It's like we've known each other forever."

I think this last comment from Mel makes a great ending line to close the interview.

"Mel, I'm afraid our time is up. I want to thank you for sharing your story with us and for such a fun morning."

"My pleasure," she replies.

Facing Todd's camera I say, "And there you have it. There's someone out there for everyone at any age. It just takes patience, a focused effort, and tenacity and your dreams can come true. This is Amanda Weyling from the *Nevada Lifestyle* Channel, and I say, "Put it out there!"

"Cut! That's a wrap!"

Meet the Authors

Nancy Buford

Nancy Buford, writing as Noëlle de Beaufort, weaves insights from her background in finance with her studies of French language, culture and literature and her love of history, travel, art and cultures into the historical romantic suspense and adventure genre. She is working on several novels delving into multiple generations of a family from its origins in France through its migration to England and beyond.

She holds a B.A. summa cum laude in French Literature from Denison University and an M.B.A. in Finance and International Business from New York University. After many years in New York City and Los Angeles, she now lives in Las Vegas with two fascinating felines.

Tina Contini

Tina Contini, writing as T.C Contin, has taught English and reading for over twenty years. She enjoys writing middle grade and young adult novels and teaching allows her ample access to her target audience. Tina is a member of The Society of Children's Book Writers and Illustrators (SCBWI), the Las Vegas Writers Group, and Writers of Southern Nevada. She is a long time resident of Las Vegas and lives there with her two wonderful children.

Steve Fey

Steve Fey was born at a very early age in the first half of the twentieth century. He spent a lot of time in childhood reading. He wrote his first story in the fourth or fifth grade. It sucked, but it was a story. One way or another he managed to spend a lifetime without writing any significant amount of fiction. Over the years he has managed a pizzeria, taught college and high school, been a technical trainer, and for a fair stretch was a computer systems person. He knows how the Internet works, and what a computer is really doing! None of which got him closer to his lifetime goal of writing fiction for a living. A few years ago he shifted gears and started living by the rule of: "Don't write anything except stuff you'd like to read." His favorite literature has always tended toward chapter books and what are now called "Young Adult" novels. Plus Mark Twain; can't forget Mark Twain. So, in spite of having read most of the "great books" this is what he now writes, mostly. The characters in the story published here are first found in a book wherein they are in fourth grade, solving crimes. He likes them as grown-ups too.

John Hill

John Hill was a full-time professional Hollywood TV and screenwriter from 1974- 1999. His credits include *Griffin and Phoenix* (1976), *Heartbeeps* (1981), co-writer of *Little Nikita* (1988) and *Quigley Down Under*, (1990). He has worked on staff as a writer-type producer on *Quantum Leap* and on *L.A. Law*, where he won an Emmy in 1991. He now teaches writing and filmmaking at the University of Nevada in Las Vegas, where he lives with his wife Nancy.

John was the winner of the 2013 *Jay MacLarty Founders Award* from the Las Vegas Writers Group.

Patricia Kranish

Pat Kranish loves living in the past. Much of her fiction is set in the Ice Age although she hates being cold and left New York seven years ago to live in Las Vegas. She has published ten wildly different stories and articles since then, inspired and encouraged by the community of writers who live and work here.

Pat lives with her husband Mike and not too far from her children who can't quite figure out what she sees in all those rocks and long dead things. She is currently working on a story based on people she knew when she was young, before they went away forever.

Trina Kurilla

A native to Las Vegas, Trina Kurilla has been a writer for as long as she can remember. With roots in poetry and short stories, she was quickly discovered by a local media studio and because of her keen attention to detail, quickly promoted to the role of lead editor. She played a crucial role in development of the feature film *Abductee* and is currently working on her first novel, a series of intertwining stories dealing with life, death, and the human connection between both. When she's not busy working with films or her own projects, she freelance edits the work of other aspiring writers.

M. McCutcheon

I have always believed that a pen/pencil is the most powerful thing a person can own. I have a love for writing. I have attended poetry readings and workshops, writing classes, and belong to Haiku on FB, and Very Bad Poetry.com. I've

self- published on Lulu.com and bothered the editors at the New Yorker. I have rejection letters from houses such as Red Hen, Glimmer Train, Missouri Review and Ragdale.

I also have a love for hot springs. I have soaked in tubs in Pittsburgh, North Carolina, Idaho, Iceland, Italy, Puerto Rico, New Mexico, and Nevada. I seek them wherever I go. The soothe of natural hot mineral water is one of the wonders of our world, in my opinion.

Marshall Prescott

Marshall Prescott served for thirty years in the law enforcement profession in Minnesota after gaining an Associate's Degree in Applied Science in Law Enforcement, and a Bachelor's Degree in Business Administration, there.

During his career, Marshall wrote detailed prisoner reports, administrative disciplinary action plans, and prisoner-rehabilitative programs, and applied for successful grant proposals to support them.

At the end of 2010, Marshall retired from law enforcement, and moved from Minnesota to Las Vegas to work on his other passion, fiction writing.

Having joined the Henderson and Las Vegas Writers' Groups which helped to complete a first draft of a crime thriller, created a children's picture book, and done freelance writing.

Marshall can be reached at marshallprescott@hotmail.com

Craig A. Ruark

Craig A. Ruark is an experienced broadcast journalist, advertising, marketing and PR professional. He provides Public Information/Public Outreach for major projects as well as marketing and advertising consultation.

In 2008, Craig became one of the first non-technical persons to become an Accredited Professional by the *U.S. Green Building Council* for 'Leadership in Energy & Environmental Design" (LEED AP). Over the past eight years he has immersed himself in the subject of "sustainability" and by combining this new knowledge with his expertise in marketing and advertising, has published a book titled "Marketing Your Green Side," which is available through Amazon.

Craig is an avid sailor, SCUBA diver, and enjoys creative writing.

Jeffrey Segal

Jeffrey Segal has taught Social Studies to middle school and high school students in Ohio, Florida, and Nevada. He writes historical and topical short stories and is a member of the Las Vegas Writers Group and Writers of Southern Nevada. He enjoys golf, Star Trek, and buffets.

Richard J. Warren

Richard Warren is an author and freelance journalist and currently the Consumer Columnist for *The Vegas Voice* newspaper. His book *Scammers, Schemers, and Dreamers*, was released in June 2014. Co-written with Elisabeth Daniels, the former head of the *Nevada Fight Fraud Task Force*, the book explores the human toll of being victimized by fraud. Richard is also the author of *A Rehabber's Tale, the Reality of Fixing and Flipping Real Estate*. Richard has written more than 150 freelance articles related to real estate investing. In 2014 his fictional short story, "Winter Crossroads," was featured in *Tales From the Silver State*, an anthology of Emerging Nevada Writers.

In addition to being the Organizer and Director of the Las Vegas Writers Group, Richard serves on the Board of Directors of the *Writers of Southern Nevada*, a non-profit organization dedicated to providing education and resources to writers. He is graduate of the University of Nevada Las Vegas having majored in English with a Concentration in Creative Writing. He is currently teaching English Composition at UNLV.

Barbra Wolfe

Barbra Wolfe moved to Las Vegas in 1993, a transplant from Manhattan and Long Beach, New York. With a BA from SUNY Stony Brook and an MBA from Baruch College, she has spent the last thirty years as a marketing executive in the financial and casino industries, and recently opened her own firm, In House Marketing LLC.

Barb is active in the Las Vegas community, has served on the boards of several local non-profits, and has received Congressional Recognition for her volunteer work.

An adventurer at heart, has climbed the Great Wall of China, soared through the air on the noses of dolphins in Mexico, danced in the streets of Rudesheim am Rhein, ridden a camel in Morocco, traveled thirty of our states and vacationed in eighteen countries so far. When not exploring the world, her favorite pastime is curling up with a good book and her rescue dog, Mila.

Meeting Billyniceguy is her debut work of fiction. She has several children's books in the works and has not totally abandoned the idea of writing juicy stories about her casino days, fictional of course.

The Las Vegas Writers Group

A Brief History

Founded by Jay MacLarty and Vic Cravello, the Las Vegas Writers Group has grown from its humble beginnings to become the premier writers group in Southern Nevada. Jay had travelled a long, hard road to publication which included 50 rejections before finally landing an agent and signing a deal with Simon & Shuster. The LVWG was a way for him to help others achieve what he had. His vision was a group that was a mix of successfully published and aspiring authors. It has grown far beyond what anyone expected.

The group, originally known as The Literati, held its first official meeting in September 2004 with four writers attending. Monthly gatherings took place in a coffee shop and the group grew slowly through word of mouth. By January of 2007 the membership had increased to the point that the meetings moved to a local pub. Establishing an internet presence through Meetup accelerated the growth rate and the group sought out a larger venue to accommodate the increasing attendance. Today membership stands at more than 300 writers with monthly meetings typically attended by 70 or more published and aspiring authors.

There are a number of reasons for the success of the group. First there is no profit motive, the meeting fee is kept as low as possible and is used to cover the cost of running the group and putting on the meetings with any excess going toward the annual holiday party and producing this anthology. Second is the quality of the monthly program. Speakers are generally individuals with something valuable to share with the members regarding both the craft and business of writing. Past presenters have included Creative Writing Faculty from UNLV, authors from major publishing houses, Emmy Award winning screenwriters, Pulitzer Prize nominees, and most recently an O' Henry Award winning writer. Lastly, and most importantly, the LVWG thrives due to the dedication of the volunteers who through there tireless efforts have helped make the group what it is today.